# ALMOST ALONE

### by Bill Muir

I0682295

# Almost Alone

## Bill Muir

### Methinx Publishing

MeThinx Publishing

If you purchase this book without a cover, you should be aware that this book may have been stolen property and reported as "unsold and destroyed" to the publisher. In such case neither the author nor the publisher has received any payment for this "stripped book."

This novel is entirely a work of fiction. The names, characters, places, and incidents portrayed in it are the work of the author's imagination. Any resemblance to actual persons, living or dead, or real events or locations, is entirely coincidental.
Copyright © Bill Muir 2011

Methinx Publishing
methinxentertainment.com

Printed in the United States of America
First paper edition by Methinx Publishing
ISBN: 978-1-7347696-2-3

Art & Design:
Contributing Editor: Kathryn Tedrick
Cover Art: Digital Coast Media, LLC

All rights reserved. No part of this book may be reproduced or transmitted in any form or by any means, electronic or mechanical, including photocopying, recording, or by any information storage and retrieval system, without written permission from the publisher. For information regarding special discounts for bulk purchases, please contact MeThinxEntertainment.com

# Chapter One

## Out of Nowhere

*Colorado, July 1856*

Alone in the farm's garden, eighteen-year-old Samantha McPherson sat on the dark, fertile soil pulling weeds. The day was hot, and she had worked hard most of the afternoon. She smiled as she stretched her arms over her head, then reached around and rubbed her aching lower back.

She wore a simple pink and white cotton dress, her long brown hair pinned up under a white straw broad-brimmed hat. Samantha, or 'Sammie,' spent every moment she could outdoors. Nothing was better than feeling the sun on her face, smelling the aroma of the pine trees, and hearing the breeze rustle through the leaves of the surrounding Aspens. The garden was one of her favorite places to be on such a beautiful day.

On the mountain, next to the farm, a tawny-red mountain lion crouched; his eyes focused on the one bright spot in the garden, the unsuspecting teenage girl. The lion's left paw extended forward before coming to rest quietly on a jagged rock. He studied his prey before continuing slowly down the mountain, always keeping her in his sight.

Sammie scooted down the row a few more feet and continued weeding. Her movement caused the lion to pause. Still hidden in the trees, he watched.

Sammie had been taught by her father to continually survey the mountainside for wild animals when she worked outside, but today she was lost in her thoughts. She wondered what her future would be; if she would ever meet someone special who would fall in love with her. What would he be like? Would he be strikingly handsome and brave? She laughed to herself. She would be happy with average looking and kind, as long as he loved her with all his heart. She would adore him and make him so happy. Nothing would make her more comfortable. But today, living on an isolated farm on the back end of a valley in Colorado, made all that seem entirely impossible.

The mountain lion continued to creep toward her. Hiding in the scattered bushes near the open field, the lion never took its eyes off its prey, sitting helpless and alone in the garden. If she fled, the lion would stop her – dead.

Sammie reached for the next weed, and as she pulled it, she uncovered a rabbit hole hidden between two carrot plants. A small brown beastie popped out and stared at her.

"Well, hello, Mrs. Rabbit. I was wondering if you were going to visit me today."

The rabbit didn't run at the sound of her words, but peacefully rubbed the back of her ears. Sammie had a way with animals, and this particular bunny visited her every time she was in the garden.

"Where are your little ones today?"

The rabbit looked at the carrot plants, seeming to decide which one to eat.

"Go ahead. You can have it. I won't tell anyone."

Suddenly, the rabbit stood up on its hind legs and sniffed the air. Its ears stood straight up, and its nose twitched. A second later, it was gone, scurrying back into its hole. Curious, Sammie looked around to see what had startled the rabbit. All Sammie saw were the trees and their long afternoon shadows lying across the hayfield.

As Sammie slid her body further down the row, the hidden lion darted from the cover of the brush and sprinted across the open field, quickly gaining speed as it ran straight for her. Nothing was going to stop him now. Even if the girl spotted him, it was too late for her to escape. The mountain lion sprinted across the open field.

Sammie sensed that something was wrong, and that feeling sent a tremor of fear through her body. Sitting up straight, she twisted her body to look to the right, nothing, and then as she turned left, her eyes locked on the charging mountain lion.

In frightened desperation, she dug her fingers into the soil and dragged her body, frantically toward her wheelchair.

"Pa! Pa! Help!"

Panicked, she pulled her eyes away from the lion and focused on reaching her chair.

"Pa!"

Sammie grabbed the wooden armrest, but in her panic, tipped over the wheelchair. She could hear the lion's low panting growls. Too frightened to look over her shoulder, she tried to push the wheelchair upright, but it was too heavy.

"Pa, help me!" She screamed.

The mountain lion made his final lunge, his teeth bared, his claws exposed.

# Chapter Two

## Family Matters

The lion flew through the air toward Sammie, as a long hunting knife sailed end over end toward the animal. A front paw touched Sammie's shoulder the same moment the blade found its mark, deep into the right side of his chest. With a final strangled yelp, the animal collapsed into a horrible heap at Sammie's side.

Benjamin, Sammie's father, raced across the garden toward his crying daughter and the dead animal.

"Are you alright, sweetheart?"

She nodded through her tears and reached out for him.

Ben lifted her into his strong arms and squeezed her tightly.

"Pa, I can't breathe."

"I'm sorry," he said, relaxing his grip.

"I don't know what's more dangerous, the lion or your hugs," Sammie teased.

"Trust me, the lion," Benjamin replied curtly.

"Maybe," she said.

Sammie wrapped her arms around his neck and kissed his tanned cheek, tears of fear still wet on her face. He had always been her best friend and hero. He loved and protected her fiercely.

Sammie's legs had never worked. A limitation that she had to bear herself. Though as a child, her father carried her everywhere as a child, they had a deep bond between them. But now, he was angry.

"Sammie, you know it's dangerous to be alone outside."

"I...I'm sorry. I know. I didn't think. I wanted to be in the garden."

"Where's your sister?" her father asked, his voice growing edgy as he carried her back to the cabin.

Sammie thought about how much she hated that her by legs that didn't work. She tried to live a normal life, but it was impossible to move around in a heavy wooden wheelchair on a farm in 1856. She often would dream of running across the hayfield or climbing a mountain, only to awaken to the reality of numb, unmoving legs. Her parents brought her to the best doctors and sought help from every source known. But by the time she was nine or ten, both her parents and Sammie had given up hope of ever walking and just accepted her fate. As a child, she would rub her legs for hours, hoping that they would wake up. They never did.

****

Inside the cabin's small bedroom, Sammie's twelve-year-old sister, Ellie, was play-acting in front of a mirror. She was dressed up in her most elegant dress, her hair curled and pinned up to perfection. In her right hand, she held a colorful, handmade paper fan.

Ellie bowed deeply in front of her imaginary audience.

"I must leave you now, for I have been invited to have dinner with the President. He is most insistent. Thank you kindly for coming to my play."

Ellen, the girl's mother, who was walking by the open door, stopped to watch her daughter. She appreciated her gift for acting and knew her daughter wanted someday, tomorrow, if possible, to be an actress in New York City.

Her mother hid her smile, "You have an imagination beyond anyone I have ever known. But shouldn't you be in the garden helping Sammie?"

Ellie stomped her foot. "Ma, you know Sammie loves being in the garden. I hate it; getting all dirty and perspiring. Besides, I've been working on a new character. Watch!"

Turning, she bent slightly at the waist and cocked her head to one side, to face her mother. Then she started twitching, shaking, and squinting as she walked toward her. "Why, Henriiii-etta! As I live and breathe, is that *you*? Goodness, you're a sight for sore eyes. How are you enjoying your life out in the country? You should have never moved from New York City to that dismal, isolated farm out west."

Her mother laughed. "Oh, you have Ms. Brough down perfectly. She was something, wasn't she? As big as the city was, she knew everything and everyone!"

Still, in character, Ellie continued. "What's that, Ellen? Got to talk in my good ear, dear. This one, right here." She pointed to her left ear and turned it toward her mother.

Both stopped when they heard banging on the front porch of the cabin.

Ellen walked to the door and quickly opened it, reaching out to Sammie in her father's arms.

"What happened?" Her mother asked.

Ben continued into the kitchen and sat Sammie at the kitchen table.

"I'll tell you what happened," Ben barked. "She was attacked by a mountain lion."

Ellen embraced her daughter, then pulled back to look into her eyes.

"Are you alright? Are you hurt?" She touched her daughter's face, lovingly smoothed her hair, then reached for a dishtowel, and dipping it into the water bucket, gently wiped the dirt and tear stains from Sammie's face.

"Sammie, what were you doing out there…alone?" The realization hit her, and she stopped to look behind her.

Knowing she could not avoid her father's wrath, Ellie had crept into the kitchen.

"Elizabeth, why weren't you with your sister? Why was she in the garden alone?" Ben asked.

"I…."

"What's wrong with you? You have no sense of responsibility. I can't depend on you for anything!" He glared at his youngest daughter and continued. "You know you're supposed to be with your sister. She can't defend herself. That's your job to watch out for just this kind of thing. How many times have I told you to go with her when she is gardening? Really, Elizabeth!"

"It's not fair!' Ellie whined. "She gets to do whatever she wants. She likes to garden, and I have to follow her around. Why can't I do what I want? Why is it my job to watch her? She always gets whatever she wants! I wish I were crippled!"

"Elizabeth! That's a terrible thing to say," her mother said in a shocked voice.

"But it's true," Ellie said, stomping off to her room.

Ben started to follow her, but his wife grabbed his arm.

"Let her be. You know this move has been hard on her. Our life here on the farm and in this cabin is much different than New York. She knows she was wrong. She'll apologize later. "

Ben trusted his wife's wisdom, and without saying another word, he left to retrieve a chicken from the coop for the evening meal. He figured the time outside preparing might help him deal with his anger.

Ben had been a successful big-city banker but itched to move to the Wild West, to work with his hands, till the land, and raise animals. He wanted to leave the crowded city and the pressure of big business behind him. He had admitted to Ellen that being confined to his small office was like living in a prison cell.

Because she loved him dearly, she agreed to sell the big house, move west, and make a living running a farm. In addition to her youngest hating the idea of leaving New York, deep in her heart Ellen also feared that the move. Living around dangerous wild animals and coping with severe weather on isolated land surrounded by Indians, Ellen feared, might just kill them. And Ellen was rarely wrong.

# Chapter Three

## Our Daily Bread

Ellen set aside her fears as she and Sammie began fixing supper. Sammie cut greens from the garden for a salad over a small low work table, while her mother cleaned potatoes at the cast iron sink. The wood-burning stove had already been stoked and started to burn hot in preparation for the bread and roasted corn that would be part of the meal.

"Sammie, I'm sorry for your sister's mean words," her mother said, breaking the silence.

"Don't blame Ellie, Ma. My handicap has affected us all."

Her mother spoke almost in prayer. "I am so sorry that you use a wheelchair, Sammie. Not a day goes by that I don't wonder, 'why you.'" She put the last potato in the water-filled pot and looked lovingly at her daughter. "I pray every day for your healing, sweetheart."

"Well," Sammie began as she turned her chair slowly toward her, ma, "I think it's a waste of time. I'm eighteen, and my legs still don't work."

"I'm not going to stop praying. God will do what He will in His time, not ours."

"You get a lot of comfort out of prayer, Ma, and that's a good thing. But don't expect me to. I just don't believe in it. I may be crippled, but your God is deaf."

"Don't say that, Sammie!"

"Why? Because it's not true or because you're afraid it *is* true?"

"God's not deaf."

"Then he doesn't have much power as you claim. Out here, Ma, we are alone. Period."

"Sammie, He is always with us."

"If He is, he's doing a lot of watching and not much doing," Sammie said, looking down at the cutting board so she wouldn't see her mother's eyes. She knew her mother had a deep faith in God and knew all too well how it hurt Ma when she talked like that. But she was tired of her unresponsive, uncaring God. She had accepted being a cripple a long time ago, why couldn't Ma?

Ellen knew it was time to be silent. Although she dearly wanted her family to grow closer to God, she was sensitive enough to know it was important that they grow toward Him on their own.

Ellie came bursting out of her room and ran over to Sammie; she wrapped her arms around her older sister and hugged her close. "I'm sorry, Sammie. I didn't mean it. You know I was just mad. I'm sorry you have to be in that stupid old chair."

"Thank you, Ellie, I know," Sammie replied.

Ellie joined in helping with the preparation of dinner.

Sammie was always quick to forgive, and in a few moments, she started singing. Her mother and sister began harmonizing with her. The beautiful music flowed through the house. Ben, with a plucked chicken in his grasp, walked into the kitchen area with a smile. He loved hearing his family sing.

As Ellen seasoned and cooked the chicken, Ellie set the table with her mother's good china, silverware, and glasses that she had brought from their home back East. Ellie added a pair of silver candlestick holders, but the candles were unlike the beautiful

tapered kind they had used in New York, these were made from beeswax, rather squat
and yellow.

With the delightful smell of perfectly roasted chicken, cobs of salted corn,
potatoes smashed and smothered in freshly churned butter, the family sat down to supper.
As usual, Ben immediately snatched some warm bread and started eating; a hard day's
work on the farm always made him hungry. Ellen cleared her throat. Looking slightly
annoyed, Ben swallowed and put down his fork. His wife smiled.

"Let's hold hands and pray. Dear Heavenly Father, we thank you for this plentiful
meal and all the good things you bring into our lives. We thank you for saving Sammie's
life today. We pray for those less fortunate than us. Amen."

Before Ellen said 'Amen,' Ben was eating again. He didn't have much use for
God, not anymore, not since God gave him a daughter with legs that didn't work. Oh,
there had been a time when he and Ellen read the Bible together and prayed. But the day
the doctors told him that his baby girl would never walk, something broke in Ben's spirit.
When he watched his girl struggle to pull herself across the rough wood floor, he felt a
part of his heart die. Ben only put up with Ellen's prayers at meals because he loved his
wife, not her God.

With a couple of bites of dinner beginning to fill his stomach, Ben spoke. "I want
to remind all three of you that you must be careful when you're outside; you especially,
Sammie. Always have a rifle with you, next to you. Understood? And nobody goes out
alone. The drought has brought wild animals further down the mountain, looking for
food. I also want you to keep an eye out Indians and trappers. This valley is lovely and
beautiful, but it is dangerous."

Ellie piped up, "I think we need to go back home to New York City."

"We *are* home," Ben replied in a stern voice.

"Well, as soon as I'm old enough, I want to move back and live with Grandma," Ellie countered.

"We'll talk about that in six years," Ben told her.

"I'll be an old lady in six years!" Ellie protested.

Everyone laughed, except Ellie.

"Enough about New York; tomorrow, your ma and I will be stacking the hay up in the rafters. It will take us most of the day," he reached over and touched Ma's arm, and she smiled back. "So, you girls need to prepare the meals and take care of the other chores on the farm."

The girls nodded.

After dinner, Sammie sat in the living room, practicing throwing a rope around a wooden calf her father had made for her. Her mother wanted to teach her lady-like things such as needlework and stitchery, but her eldest daughter preferred being a bit of a tomboy. To do as many real things as she could, as much as physically possible. Ellen thought perhaps this was a way of compensating for being so limited in her chair.

As Sammie threw the rope over and over, perfecting her skill, her thoughts were back in the garden. She had been genuinely foolish, daydreaming, and not paying attention. What if Pa had missed or been ten seconds too late? The lion would have seized her by the throat and killed her, or worse, maimed her even more. The thought made her shiver.

"Are you alright, Sammie?" Ma asked. She knew her daughter and that in this

14

quietness, she was most likely reliving those terrifying moments that morning.

"Fine, Ma. Just got a little chill."

Sammie smiled and rolled closer to the fire, her mind returning to the attack and what could have happened. She knew she had a pretty face, what if the lion had scarred her, or blinded her? Indeed, there would be no chance of a man in her life if that happened. Oh, how stupid she was. She had to pay attention, be aware, carry a rifle. What if she had died? One death in the family was enough. They had lost her younger brother, Joshua, years ago, back in New York to whooping cough. Another would kill her father. And her mother? She wasn't sure. Her Ma's faith, although Sammie herself didn't believe, sometimes was the most certain thing in the family. Sammie stopped to look at the people she loved.

On the other side of the small room, Ellie sang and danced to no one in particular, but still performing, while Ben silently whittled a small chunk of wood. She wondered if he was thinking of that morning and was blaming her for the events that transpired.

Suddenly Ma appeared, from the kitchen. Placing her hands on her hips, she said teasingly, "I have one daughter who wants to be a cowboy and another one who wants to be an actress, but no daughters who want to help me clean up."

Both girls looked up and followed her into the kitchen. Ellie mimicked her mother's walk and repeated her last line, sounding precisely like her ma.

****

The voice of the farm's rooster broke the early morning stillness. Sammie woke and greeted the day with a smile. Her hand reached over and pushed open the bedroom window to the sound of birds singing. She loved the smell of the early morning mountain air. Leaning out the small window, she looked up at the blue sky, not a cloud in sight.

"This is going to be another perfect day," Sammie told a nearby bluebird sitting on a horse post. He turned his head to look at her, seemed to nod his head in agreement, and then flew off.

Sammie leaned back inside and still on her bed, slipped on the fresh clothes her Ma had set on a small table by the bed. With her sister still asleep next to her, Sammie quietly slid into her wheelchair. She spun the chair around and began pushing the heavy wooden wheels with her hands. She was embarrassed by how callous her hands were from pushing herself around. *What boy would ever want to hold these ugly, calloused hands?* She thought. She put her hands in her lap and laughed. *Calluses and a wheelchair. The perfect dream girl.*

Sammie went out on the porch and then into the yard to enjoy the tranquility of early morning with its crisp air, spotless skies, and the sweet fragrance from the flowers planted along the porch. Mornings were her favorite time. She looked over the beautiful valley where her family had settled and smiled. She leaned back in the wheelchair and let the warm sun blanket her tanned face.

The sound of her parent's laughing caused her to look across the yard toward the barn. She admired how much her parents were still in love. After all these years, her ma always adored her pa. And her pa still loved and admired her mother. Sammie could feel the energy between them. They were soul mates forever. Their on-going romance was what made Sammie want someone in her life. A man like her pa: kind, reliable, hard-working, a man who liked to laugh, and who only had eyes for her.

Sammie watched ma pulling down on a thick rope hanging from a pulley that was

16

hitched to the roof of the barn. With each pull on the rope, a massive bale of hay slowly rose toward the large opening above the double doors of the barn. The opening led to the loft. Her mother, with her big beautiful smile, leaned out of the opening and seeing Sami blew a kiss before pulling the bale of hay inside.

She closed her eyes, reflecting on this moment; parents who loved each other, her funny little sister, the farm, and the animals. Sammie couldn't contain her joy.

Suddenly, from inside the barn, she heard a chilling scream, then a thump. She watched her father race into the barn, and in a moment, she heard him scream. She had never heard her father cry.

"Sammie, bring towels! Your Ma fell from the loft," he yelled from inside the barn.

"Pa!"

"Hurry, she's bleeding. I think she's hurt bad. "

****

# Chapter Four

## The Accident in the Barn

Sammie struggled to push her wheelchair toward the cabin, but the ruts in the yard from the wagon made it difficult. She wished she could run like everyone else. Inside the cabin, she grabbed several towels, and as she made her way back out called to her sister, who was still in bed.

"Ellie, Ma's been hurt. Fill a bucket with water and meet me in the barn!"

Sammie was halfway to the barn when her sister came running out of the cabin, still in her nightshirt.

"Ellie! Stop right now and get that water. If Ma's bleeding, we can't do much without water to clean the wounds."

Ellie stopped, clearly torn between getting to her mother as fast as possible and going back for the water.

"Hurry!" their father yelled, "She's bleeding badly."

His words made Ellie's decision. She ran back for the water.

Sammie entered the barn and found her parents on the dirt floor. Her mother flat on her back, and her father draped over her. She knew this was bad as she moved toward her mother's motionless body, and she couldn't help looking up at the high loft from where her mother had fallen.

She pushed herself from her wheelchair, sliding to the floor. Her father's panicked face, and his tears nearly broke her heart. She could not allow her mother's broken body to affect her the same way. Her mother needed her like a patient needs a calm doctor in

18

an emergency.

"I should carry her into the house and lay her on the bed." Sammie's muscular father slid his arms under his wife, but her screams of agony stopped him.

"Don't," his daughter said sternly. "If she broke her back, Pa, you could paralyze her."

"Help her, Sammie. Please," her father begged.

All of Sammie's life, her father had been the strong one, the brave ones, the decisive one, but not today. For the first time, Sammie was stronger than her Pa.

Sammie gently examined her unconscious mother, checking the large gash on her head and looking for broken bones. As she did, Ellie ran into the barn, splashing water as she went. Setting the bucket down near her sister, she took one look and became hysterical.

Ellen's lips started to move. She was trying to say something to Sammie, but she couldn't hear her mother over Ellie's wailing.

"Pa, please calm Ellie down. I can't hear what Ma is saying."

Taking the younger girl from the barn would have been ideal, but Ben could not leave his wife's side. So he took Ellie in his arms and stroked her back, whispering words of comfort he knew were false.

"I can't feel my legs," Ellen whispered.

As Sammie finished the examination, her mother began to pray in a painful, halting whisper that shook her to the core. It took all her mental strength to remain calm and not give in to hysterics like her sister. Dipping a dish towel into the water, she applied it to the large open wound on the side of her mother's head. She was bleeding a lot.

"Ma, I know your head and back hurt something awful. I have to tie this towel tightly around your head to stop the bleeding. It's going to hurt even worse. I'm sorry," Sammie whispered.

Ellen looked into Sammie's eyes and saw the seriousness of her injuries reflected there. Nodding slightly, she tried to squeeze her daughter's hand, but she didn't have the strength. Then closing her eyes, she inhaled a shaky breath and continued to pray.

Sammie leaned close to her mother's ear. "Ma, I think you broke your back."

"Oh, dear God, help me," her mother gasped.

Straightening up, Sammie turned to her father. "Pa, I need you to find a board-wide and long enough to slip under her so we can take her to the house."

It took some doing, but Ben found some boards the right length. His hands shook as he worked, laying out four boards side-by-side and then fastening them together using three shorter cross boards. When he was finished, he secured a rope to one end and dragged the improvised stretcher over to his wife.

"Ellie, you'll have to help me," Ben said.

Ellie knelt in the dirt next to her mother, wanting to help.

"We need to do this slowly and carefully, so we don't cause any further damage to her back," Sammie instructed them.

Ben and Ellie looked at Sammie, waiting for instructions.

"You must slide the board under her, Pa, while Ellie and I gently ease her up a little at a time." She looked down at her mother. "I'm sorry, Ma, this is going to hurt."

"Do what you have to do," her mother replied bravely.

It was slow and agonizing Ellen tried not to scream, but she couldn't prevent the deep moans from escaping her lips. Tears streaked down the faces of all four as they worked. When they finally had her in place, Ben tied some of the longer towels together to secure Ellen on the makeshift stretcher. They couldn't risk having her fall off when they pulled her back to the cabin.

As they slowly dragged the stretcher out of the barn, Ellen couldn't help screaming out in pain.

# Chapter Five

## Council in the Cabin

The trip from the barn to the cabin felt like an eternal nightmare to Sammie. She felt upset for her mother and so helpless. Her mind churned with questions. Why would God allow this to happen? Why her ma and not somebody cruel or evil? If this was how God treated someone who believed and loved him, what kind of a God was he? Sammie just didn't understand her mother's God, not at all.

Sweating more from fear than exertion, Ben tried to avoid any bumps, but the uneven ground made the task impossible. Ellen cried out with every jolt, no matter how small. Things went smoother when they dragged the board up the wheelchair ramp to the porch. Ellie held the door open as her father pulled the stretcher into the cabin. By the time they were in the center of the room, Ellen was once again unconscious.

"Ma! Ma!" Ellie cried out.

Ben also panicked, but Sammie quickly checked her mother's heartbeat and breathing. "She passed out from the pain. It's better this way. We can move her easier."

"Then I'm taking her into the bedroom," Ben said, reaching for the rope again.

"Yes, while she's unconscious," Sammie agreed, "but she must remain on the board."

Later, Ellen awoke on her bed, still partially tied to the stretcher. She opened her eyes as the pain came back full-blown, and she turned her head to the side and threw up. Ellie cleaned up the floor and bed while Sammie gently cleaned her mother and helped her rinse her mouth with water. Then she placed a cold, wet cloth on her mother's

22

forehead.

"Why didn't I think of this sooner," Ben said suddenly, as he ran from the room. He came back with a bottle of laudanum, a potent pain killer, and it was the only available medication of its kind that did not require a doctor's prescription.

His wife made a face as she swallowed a spoonful of the bitter-tasting stuff. Before long, she was fast asleep. Gently, Sammie removed the blood-soaked towel from around her head and cleaned the wound with warm soap and water. The gash was deep, but the bleeding had stopped. Then she placed a fresh, clean folded piece of linen over the injury, and carefully wrapped another piece of linen around her ma's head to hold the dressing in place. When she finished, she kissed her mother on the cheek and motioned her Pa to follow her.

"Best, we let her sleep. Let's go in the other room."

Ellie had collapsed in a tight little ball in a chair, her arms around her knees, looking scared. Still, in her bloodstained nightshirt, Ben picked her up and put her in his lap, as Sammie rolled her chair up next to him. She took his large hand in her small one and squeezed it to comfort him.

As the three sat there, exhausted, Sammie looked around the room. It no longer felt the way it had last night. It seemed empty and hollow without her mother's presence. The sadness crept slowly into her heart and lodged there like a lump of black tar. She looked at her father and sister and realized they were in shock and numb. So, Sammie gathered her strength, swallowed her fear, and spoke to them quietly.

"Ma is in bad shape," she began.

"I know," Ben whispered, almost afraid to admit it out loud.

Ellie sat up and pulling up her knees; she again wrapped her arms around them. With a shaky sigh, she finally stopped crying to listen.

"I'll have to take her to the doctor in the next town," Ben continued.

"But that's so far away, Pa. The trip will be agonizing for Ma," Sammie said.

"What choice do we have?" Ben asked, frustrated. "If she doesn't receive proper medical care, she'll never be able to leave that bed again. She might even die from complications."

"Even with a doctor, she may be bedridden for the rest of her life, Pa." Sammie hated saying that, but she had to prepare her father and sister for the worst-case scenario. Ben turned his head to look at his daughter. "I will make sure she receives whatever treatment she needs. We'll leave in the morning at first light. You girls will need to pack a few of your things for the trip. Sammie, pack some things for your Ma."

"How will all of us fit in the wagon?" Ellie asked.

Ben seemed confused for a moment and then shook his head. "I'm…, I'm sorry. I'm not thinking this through. We can't abandon the farm." Ben stopped and looked at his two daughters, again shook his head and frowned.

"You girls will have to stay."

"No! Sammie can stay. I want to be with Ma."

Ben ignored Ellie's outburst and continued, "It will take us three or four days to get to town, probably longer with your Ma in the back of the wagon. Then we'll have the same trip back. Another factor that complicates things is time. We don't know what the doctor will say or how long we'll have to stay in town. The animals need to be fed and watered. Otherwise, we'll lose them all. We can't afford that. Your ma wouldn't want

24

that."

Sammie knew her father was right, but she also recognized that in a wheelchair, she could never handle the job of managing the farm chores alone. There was too much physical work. Ellie would also have to stay and help. Ben knew that too.

"Ellie. You have to stay here."

"Ma is more important than a stupid farm and stupid animals," Ellie shouted.

"Of course she is, but there's nothing you girls can do for your ma along the way."

"Who cares if we lose the farm? We can move back to New York City, where we belong. I hate this place! If we hadn't moved here, Ma would never have fallen."

Ellie's words cut her father to the bone.

"We can't leave the animals, Ellie, they'll die," Sammie said.

"Fine! You take care of the animals, but I'm going with Ma! "

She pushed herself out of her father's lap, stood, and turned toward them, her arms crossed in defiance, eyes glaring.

Ben shook his head. "Ellie, you need to remain here and help your sister. She can't stay here alone."

"I'm not staying here. Sammie will just have to go, too," Ellie insisted.

"No, I'm sorry, Ellie," Ben said firmly. "I have to depend on both of you to keep things going here." Seeing the stubborn look on his younger daughter's face, he continued. "We should only be gone a short time, and when we get back, everything will go back to normal."

"No!" Ellie stomped her foot and stormed off to her room.

****

That evening, Sammie took off her mother's blood-stained dress, washed her lovingly with warm soapy water, and then dressed her in loose, comfortable travel clothes. She changed the head bandage, then gathered the stained clothing from everyone, and set them in a washbasin to soak. Her ma stirred, and Sammie gave her another dose of laudanum to get her through the night. While Sammie cared for her mother, Ben prepared for the early morning trip. He bathed in the small bathroom and put on clean clothes, then joined Sammie at his wife's bedside. Although the medicine helped, her pain was unbearable at times, and she would awaken. Her prayers were barely audible, but they both knew she was praying. Sammie didn't know what felt worse: her ma's pain or praying to an uncaring, callous, unreliable God.

At one point during the night, Ellen asked Sammie to read from her Bible. Ben eased to his feet and went for the Bible. He returned and handed it to Sammie without a word or expression on his face. Sammie looked into her father's eyes and tried to figure out what he was thinking. She had no idea and was afraid to ask.

"Where should I read from, Ma?" Sammie whispered.

"Psalm 23, sweetheart," she said.

Sammie had a hard time finding Psalms since she had never opened the book. Looking in the index, she found the right place and gently turned the pages in the big book.

Sammie began, " 'The Lord is my shepherd, I shall not want. He makes me lie down in green pastures. He leads me beside quiet waters. He restores my soul. He guides me in the paths of righteousness for His name's sake. Even though I walk through the valley of the shadow of death, I will fear no evil, for thou art with me.' "

Sammie looked at her mom, now peacefully asleep. With her hand still on the open Bible, Sammie lowered her head and wept.

# Chapter Six

## Leaving the Girls Alone

The next morning, Sammie rose before sunrise to fix breakfast. As she made coffee and cooked a pot of oatmeal, she heard her parents talking in the next room.

"No, we can't leave the girls alone. We have to stay here. Sammie can take care of me," her mother said. "She's smart and knows a lot about medical care."

"She does," Benjamin agreed, "but she's not a doctor. We must see a doctor. Your injuries are too critical, and I won't take a chance, Ellen. We are going into town tomorrow to see the doctor."

Ellen tried to shift to a more comfortable position and cried out. She knew her husband was right.

"I guess we have no choice," she admitted in a defeated voice.

"Rest while Sammie gets your breakfast. I'll start packing. We need to leave as soon as possible."

Sammie took breakfast to Ellen but realized she couldn't sit up to eat. She slowly gave her mother several small sips of water, as much as she could get down.

"Don't worry, sweetheart. I'm not hungry." Her mother smiled at Sammie's efforts. "I'm sorry all of this has to fall on you, Sammie. It's not fair, but I know I can trust you to keep things going and take care of your little sister."

"It's okay, Ma. We'll manage. It's only for a short time. You'll be back in a few days. Ellie and I will be fine. Don't worry."

"You do have that strong McPherson blood," she smiled and then caught her breath as pain again startled her. "We'll be back as soon as possible, and I'll pray that God protects you both."

Sammie was about to contradict her mother but bit back the bitter words she would have otherwise said out loud. *Why would He even bother? Where was He when you fell?* She knew her mother would have explained that God doesn't make bad things happen. They just happened, but that He walked with us through them. If praying gave her mother comfort, then she wasn't going to take that small bit of relief away from her with questions.

After taking her mother's breakfast dishes into the kitchen, Sammie woke up Ellie, and they joined their father in the kitchen for breakfast. No one felt like eating, but Ben knew he had a long trip ahead of him and needed the nourishment. Sammie also ate because she had a full day of chores ahead of her. But Ellie barely picked at her food. She sat at the table sullen and pouting. Finally, she threw down her spoon.

"I want to see Ma."

When Ellie went into the room and saw her mother's drawn ashen face, she realized Ma was still in horrible pain, and she cried and begged to go with them. But, Ellen refused to give in.

"Sammie will need your help more than ever. There's too much work to be done for her to do it alone, especially with her...." Her mother's words faded away as worry and pain once more took over. It would be hard enough for two girls to handle everything themselves. Sammie's handicap made the task doubly hard. Ellen closed her eyes. There was no easy solution. If only she hadn't leaned so far out trying to grab that hay - if she hadn't fallen - now her whole family was in jeopardy.

After finishing his breakfast in the kitchen, Ben went outside to hitch up the wagon, using two of his three horses. He pulled up next to the ramp from the porch. Sammie placed the basket with food on her lap and wheeled outside while Ellie carried a small suitcase with her parents' clothing. Ben carried out two small barrels of water, which he then lashed down tightly in the back of the wagon. After that, he fetched two full water canteens, and some dried fruit tied in a big handkerchief. He put one container in the back next to Ellen's bedroll, and the other under his seat, along with the fruit.

The three went back inside to bring Ellen out to the wagon. The morning's spoonful of laudanum would help somewhat, but they all knew that moving Ellen would be terrible. They lowered her to the floor. Then Ben carefully lifted one end of the boards and slowly dragged her to the front door. Sammie felt helpless. She hated now more than ever that she had to use a wheelchair.

Ellie helped her dad slide the stretcher through the front door and down the ramp. Perspiration covered Ellen's face. She held back her screams from her daughters, but the look on her face gave away the pain she was experiencing.

Ben slid one end of the stretcher onto the wagon bed and raced to the other end to lift it and slide it on.

Once everything was situated as well as possible, Ben turned to face Sammie.

"You're an intelligent young woman. I love and trust you completely, and I know you'll keep things running smoothly. Keep your rifle nearby at all times."

He turned to Ellie. "I know you'd rather come with us, sweetheart, but I really need you here. You must help your sister."

He then took a moment to gather his thoughts as he looked around the farm and then back at both of the girls.

"Remember, the farm will be vulnerable, as will you. Watch out for dangerous animals, Indians, and trappers. I'm sorry we have to leave you alone, but I promise we'll be back as soon as possible. And Sammie, I'm sorry I didn't have time to stock up more provisions. There just wasn't time."

Sammie assured him. "It's August with plenty of crops coming in. We'll make do."

Ben hugged both girls before climbing up on the seat of the wagon. His hands reached over and lifted the reins from the wooden hand break.

"Take care of each other, girls," their mother called out bravely. "I love you."

"We love you, too, Ma," Sammie called.

Ellie was crying too much to say anything as the wagon pulled away. She ran after it down the hill, calling out, "take me with you!"

Hearing Ellie's cries, Benjamin pulled on the reins to stop the wagon. When Ellie caught up to him, he turned toward his youngest with a stern expression. "Ellie, you go on back to your sister right *now*. You'll be thirteen in a few days, so you're not a little girl anymore. Ma and I are depending on you, so stop that crying immediately. Time is against us, and you're not helping one bit. Your Ma has enough to deal with. She doesn't need to be fretting over your childish antics. Now go! Go back to the farm."

Ellie stared at her Pa as she brushed the tears from her cheeks. She watched, trembling, as he turned away from her. With a shout to the horses, he drove away, never looking back even once.

She stood rooted to the spot until the last particle of dust disappeared over the

31

ridge. Then with a heavy, hollow heart, she started walking back to the farm. *I'm not selfish,* Ellie said to herself, *I just don't want to be left alone, with only Sammie.* Fear and anger started building within her. *It isn't fair. It just isn't fair!*

As Ellie headed back to the cabin, her tirade continued, and Sammie could hear her say, "We need to go. I don't *care* about this stupid old farm. I don't care what happens to the animals, either. I want to go!"

As she stomped past her sister to go inside, Sammie heard her mutter. "If you weren't in that wheelchair, I could have gone with them."

Ellie's words stung. And although Sammie knew that things would be difficult while her parents were away, she had no idea just how difficult life would become.

****

Benjamin hated being so stern with Ellie, but what choice did he have? He loved his daughters…both his daughters. However, his youngest seemed to be taking her time growing up, and out here in the wilderness, it was a luxury he couldn't afford to give her. He looked back at his wife. The painful grimace on her face seemed permanent. Even in sleep, it was always there as though the pain followed her into unconsciousness. Glancing back to the road ahead, he couldn't erase the fear in the pit of his stomach.

*Will she survive?* He asked himself. *And if she does, will she be paralyzed for the rest of her life? Will the girls be able to take care of themselves and the farm without me?* He was full of self-doubt. *I should have put up more food for the animals.*

He continued down the road a spell, seeing little but the dirt road ahead of him. The guilt gnawed through his thoughts. *It's my fault that Ma fell. She shouldn't have been working in the barn. I should have hired some help instead of asking her to do a man's*

32

*work.*

A soft voice cut into his thoughts, "The accident wasn't your fault, Ben. You know that. I was careless, acting like we were newlyweds again, and that's why I lost my balance. We'll be fine. I'll be fine. God will take care of the girls and us."

"Is mind reading one of your many talents, now?" He tried to tease her and make her laugh, make the statement funny, but he failed miserably.

"Ohhh," Ellen gasped as the wagon bounced over a rut. "Can we go slower, please? Oh, God, please help Ben. Clear the road ahead of us and protect us. We know you have me in your hands. Oh, please, God, the pain. "

Suddenly he felt very bitter. *God? How could she bring up God? Obviously, he's too busy to watch out for one of his most devoted believers. If there is a God, he really doesn't care. I'll take care of you and the girls,* he thought with frustration. *Because this God you think so highly of isn't doing such a great job.* Slowing the horse's pace, he looked back again at Ellen, her eyes closed, and her sweet face pinched in pain. She was asleep, no, probably unconscious. Either way, he urged the horses to a faster clip. He had to get her to a doctor and fast.

They traveled all day, and just before dusk became complete darkness, Ben found a suitable spot to camp for the night. After settling the horses, he gathered wood for a small campfire, made coffee, and something to eat. When it was finished, the loving husband climbed into the back of the wagon. He carefully fed Ellen, although she didn't have much of an appetite, then he ate the rest. Sitting next to her, he held her hand and watched her face until she fell asleep. Eventually, he slept too, still sitting with his back to the front of the wagon.

# Chapter Seven

## The Moccasins

Sammie remained on the dirt road until the dust from the family wagon settled to the ground. Her eyes slowly surveyed the farm as if looking for God. If there was a God, she hoped He was in the wagon with her mom.

Sammie sat there thinking of the large farm and the task of keeping it alive while her parents were gone. She felt small and incapable. Her mother had always spoken hope into Sammie's life, and now she wondered where she would find that hope. For the next several days, she was going to have to live without her ma or pa. She had never done that before, not even for a day. The responsibility of the farm rested solely on her, and she didn't think that was the right place for it to be.

Sammie pushed herself up the hill to the cabin. She could hear Ellie crying inside and felt sorry for her. Like most sisters, they didn't always get along. They were opposites in almost every way. Ellie was an actress, Sammie, a caregiver. Ellie was emotional while Sammie was a thinker. Ellie was a scatter-brain in Sammie's eyes; Sammie was too severe and bossy, according to Ellie.

But Sammie loved her sister, and she knew that their parents' leaving was even more difficult for Ellie. She went inside to comfort her. Sammie settled her chair next to her sister, lying on her mother's bed, and softly caressed her hair.

"I'm sorry about what has happened," Sammie said tenderly.

Her sister looked up, and Sammie saw a deep sadness in her eyes. Ellie had no words. So she simply laid her head back down on the pillow and continued to weep.

"Stay here until you feel better. Then come outside," Sammie said kindly.

Sammie turned in her wheelchair and left the room. She was now going to have to do the morning chores alone. Sammie spent the rest of the morning taking care of the chickens, milking the cows, feeding the pigs, and tending to the goats. When she stopped to eat lunch, she thought it would be a good idea to pack a basket lunch and take Ellie down to the lake. Sammie thought a swim and picnic might take her sister's mind off the tragedy and their parents' absence.

**** 

The afternoon breeze made the leaves of the Aspen trees dance. The waterfall spilled crystal clear into the almost still blue lake. Sammie sat on a blanket against the trunk of a 60-foot pine tree, soaking in the sun and watching her sister swim. She was still trying to make sense of it all. One misstep and everything had changed for them in a second. She was sorting through the last 24 hours when she saw Ellie climb out of the water.

Pulling her wet hair behind her ears and wringing the water out, she joined her sister on the blanket in the shade of the tree. The two of them enjoyed their sandwiches and reminisced about better times. Ellie talked about sitting around the fireplace during a snowy winter day playing charades. Sammie told Ellie about the night she and her father played chess almost till dawn after both Ellie and Ma had gone to bed.

Suddenly Sammie felt as if someone or something was watching them. She twisted her upper body and scanned the nearby trees that covered the mountainside all the way down to the water. She didn't see anything suspicious, but she couldn't shake the feeling that they were not alone.

She reached out and grabbed the rifle on the blanket, and put it on her lap.

"What's wrong, Sammie," Ellie asked.

"I think someone or something is watching us."

"Do you think it's another mountain lion?"

"I don't know," Sammie confessed. "I just feel like we're being watched."

Ellie stood up and looked around. When she didn't see anything out of place, she shrugged. "It's probably nothing."

"I think we should head back to the house."

"No, Sammie, I want to swim some more," Ellie insisted.

Sammie started gathering up the food and putting things in the basket.

"It's nothing! I'll look around to make sure." Before Sammie could stop her, Ellie started toward the dense forest lining the lake.

"*No!* Ellie, come back."

Her sister completely ignored her and headed toward the grove of trees. Although Ellie was scared, she didn't want Sammie to know. She was going to prove that she wasn't a little baby and didn't need her sister to take care of her.

"Ellie, please don't go in there," Sammie called again, pulling herself up into the wheelchair. "Stop!"

"It's just your imagination. Don't worry."

"Ellie, stop!"

"You're not my Ma; you're just my sister," Ellie said spitefully, as she turned and stepped past the tree line.

Ellie had done this a thousand times. She would go into the forest without anything happening. She stopped every once in a while to look around. Nothing. She turned around and started to walk back when she noticed a pair of moccasins on the ground next to a tree. She looked around but didn't see anyone. She had no idea that the Indian, the moccasins belonged to, was hiding only a few feet away. Not one muscle moved on his healthy body.

Leaning over, Ellie scooped up the moccasins.

She walked back to Sammie with her arms behind her back. When she reached the blanket, she raised her arms with a triumphant smile, to show off the moccasins hanging from her hand.

"Sammie, look what I found."

Sammie went pale.

"Where did you get those?"

"I found them over there," Ellie said, pointing back the way she had come. "Imagine an Indian running off and leaving his shoes."

"I don't imagine they would," Sammie looked around, trying to see if she could find the owner of the moccasins.

Ellie looked back at the trees.

"No, there's no one there. I looked," Ellie argued.

"Yes, there is. Slowly stand next to me. Indians are great at hiding. If they don't want to be seen, you won't see them."

Sammie studied the trees, holding the rifle in her hands.

"Carefully place the basket and blanket on my lap, but don't jar the rifle. Leave those moccasins here. Let's get back to the cabin. Now!" Sammie whispered authoritatively.

The girls hurried back to the house. Ellie pushed her sister's wheelchair across the ground toward the cabin as Sammie held the rifle, cocked, scanning the woods and focusing on every small moment. She saw no one.

The Indian never moved and never took his eyes off them. He'd been watching this family for some time. He knew what had happened to their mother, and he knew the two sisters were alone, helpless, and unprotected.

# Chapter Eight

## Farm Girls

Once they reached the house, Sammie had one more look back before entering the cabin. When she realized Ellie still had the moccasins, she swallowed her frustration and instructed her to leave them out on the porch.

Inside the cabin, Sammie locked up everything. The truth was that she didn't know what to do other than hiding. In all the years of living on the farm, they had never seen an Indian. The only time she had seen Indians was in a museum painting in New York. Sammie now realized that although her father had taught her to fear Indians, he had never shown her exactly how to deal with them.

Sammie bemoaned her situation, the same day her parents had to leave; she discovers that there's an Indian close to the cabin. She touched her hair; a reaction to the thought of being scalped was so strong that her hand moved involuntarily to the top of her head.

That night, after Ellie went to bed early, partly from being bored by having to stay inside and partly from being emotionally exhausted by her ma's accident. Sammie stayed up to clean the kitchen.

Her chair in front of the sink, she struggled with the feeling of being so totally alone. There was no one. She began to cry. Although she did it softly so that Ellie wouldn't hear, just like her father, Sammie believed crying was a weakness.

After cleaning the kitchen, she rolled over to the sitting area next to the lantern on a small table. She had thought about reading but was too tired.

She lowered the wick in the lantern, putting out the flame. She was about to go to bed but decided just to sit in the darkness since the room, and her soul felt the same way – dark. She was thinking about what tomorrow would be like when she noticed movement outside the front window. She sat motionless in the darkness and stared outside, hoping the moonlight would reveal who or what was there.

Then Sammie heard soft footsteps on the porch, each step bringing the uninvited guest closer to the door. When Sammie realized the door wasn't locked, her body tightened, her hands turned into fists. Someone was moving toward the unlocked front door.

She slowly rolled forward, trying to make as little noise as possible, as the footsteps moved closer. She was afraid that whoever was on the porch would reach the door before she did, the door banging open, and someone or something lunging at her.

Sammie reached the door and threw her arm out, sliding a narrow piece of wood across the latch, locking it. As she moved back into the dark room, she saw the shadow again through the window, and deftly retrieved her rifle from the kitchen table. Then alert, determined, and scared, she parked her chair facing the window.

It wasn't long before, in the quiet darkness, Sammie fell asleep. She never saw the face peering through the window, into the darkened room.

**** 

When the rooster crowed the next morning, Sammie awoke with a start, disoriented in her wheelchair, and tired to the bone. She felt like she'd hardly slept despite the truth that she had fallen asleep many times while trying to stay up and guard the cabin. Yesterday's events had gotten the best of her. Nevertheless, she scolded herself for dozing off.

Now awake, she poured cold water from the pitcher and washed the sleep from her eyes. Sammie started breakfast and called for her sister to wake up. The two girls sat quietly at the table.

Sammie broke the silence. "After we finish cleaning up, why don't we go to the barn and do the morning chores?"

Ellie shrugged.

Sammie carefully thought through what she should tell her little sister. *What would Ma do? How would Pa protect us if he were here?* She had no answer. *God help me,* she thought again, and then laughed to herself. No help there, she was on her own.

"While we're outside today, we need to be alert and to keep an eye on each other." Sammie paused and looked at Ellie, demanding her attention. "I saw someone on the porch last night."

Ellie looked up at her sister, her interest piqued. "The Indian?"

"I think so."

"What did he do?" she asked, breathless with a combination of fear and excitement.

"He came up to the porch, maybe just to look around. I did notice that his moccasins were gone."

"Is that all you think he wanted?"

"I think he knows we are here alone, Ellie. We're vulnerable until Pa and Ma get back. We need to watch out for each other and stay together."

Before leaving the cabin, Sammie laid her rifle across her lap.

Inside the barn, Sammie spotted her mother's bloody bonnet on the wooden floor. Making sure her sister wasn't watching, she quickly scooped it up and tucked it next to her in the wheelchair.

"I'll milk Daisy because I know how much you hate it," Sammie said.

"I'll gather the eggs."

Sammie gave her sister space, not talking too much or giving her instructions.

****

The barn chores took all morning, and the noontime meal was a welcome break. That afternoon they went to the garden to pick the ripe vegetables and do some hoeing.

Ellie dug up potatoes and turnips, while Sammie picked beans and corn. Ellie finished filling a basket with vegetables and was about to begin another when she heard an ominous sound. Curious, she turned lazily toward the sound and froze.

The blood drained from her face as she stared into a rattlesnake's unblinking eyes. It was coiled up, and its triangular head was raised, ready to strike. Its tongue flicked out at her with an almost hypnotic rhythm.

"Sammie?" Her voice was not loud, sounding more like a squeak, but it immediately caught her sister's attention.

Sammie looked up. As soon as she saw her sister, her eyes caught the movement of the snake. The rattlesnake was only three feet away, its extended body weaving back and forth in a frightful pre-strike pose. Fear shot through her like a spike of adrenaline. Forcing herself to remain calm and focused, Sammie slowly raised her rifle and aimed at the snake. There was no room for error. If she missed, it might scare the reptile off, but it also might strike her sister first.

Her Pa's words came back to her. *Hold the gun steady and sight your target down the length of the barrel. Then gently squeeze the trigger.* Following his instructions to the letter, Sammie aimed at the snake's head and pulled the trigger.

A scream erupted from Ellie's throat as the snake's head darted forward, but then fell to the ground as the bullet hit its target. Ellie ran to her sister and threw herself into her arms. Sammie took the breath she'd been holding, and held Ellie for all she was worth.

"Are you alright?" Sammie asked, trying not to shake as she soothed and hugged her little sister. She looked over Ellie's shoulder at the dead snake. *That was close,* she thought, *too close.*

Once both girls calmed down, Ellie stood up straight and wiped the tears from her face. She then went over to look at the giant, dangerous, but dead snake.

"You saved me, Sammie! Wait till Pa hears about this. You shot that rattlesnake dead."

**** 

Later that night, Sammie and Ellie went to bed but were too tired to fall asleep. The two of them lay awake, staring at the ceiling.

The girls shared one room and a full-sized bed. A pine wardrobe and a small matching four-drawer dresser their Pa had made, held their clothing and personal items. There was plenty of room for Sammie to move around in her wheelchair. Their Ma had made a beautiful quilt that covered the bed and a large, round rug that matched the floor. A lantern sat on the dresser, casting shadows around the room as small blasts of wind from the storm outside blew through cracks in the log walls.

"Thanks for saving my life today," Ellie said with genuine gratefulness in her voice.

"That's nice of you to say. I would do it again, you know, because I love you, Ellie McPherson."

"I love you too," she whispered back, " I haven't been very helpful, have I? I'm sorry. I'll be better."

"You know, we're McPherson women. We can handle anything – together."

Ellie smiled at her big sister and cuddled up next to her. "I'm glad you're my big sister," she said. And as Sammie put her arms around Ellie, she hoped they wouldn't have to prove her statement.

The sound of breaking glass abruptly ended their thoughts and filled them with fear.

# Chapter Nine

## The Intruder

"What was that?" Ellie's voice croaked.

"I think it was the front window breaking." Sammie slipped into her chair and looked around the room.

"Oh no," she whispered. "It's not here!"

Ellie bolted out of bed and stood beside her sister. "What's not here?"

"My rifle. I think I left it on the kitchen table." Sammie felt very foolish, especially after the incident on the porch. *How could I be so stupid?*

This scared Ellie more than anything, but she had to remain quiet and brave. " What do you think is out there?"

"Maybe the Indian," Sammie said, whispering.

Ellie's eyes grew large with fear. "What does he want? Do you think he'll hurt us?"

"I don't know," Sammie admitted. Then she squared her shoulders in determination. "Not if I can help it. Ellie, please, stay by the bed,"

She quietly rolled to the door and pressed her ear against it.

She could hear the sound of nails clicking against the floor. It wasn't an Indian. Some animal was inside the house, probably looking for food. Sammie hoped it wasn't a black bear. Then she heard clawing in the kitchen, most likely against the pantry door. Sammie listened as the animal walked around the room.

"Sniff, sniff, chuff!"

It was coming closer.

"Sniff, sniff."

The sound was coming from under the door. Sammie jerked back.

"It's not an Indian," Sammie said, her voice low, but no longer a whisper. "It's an animal. It can smell us. It knows we're here."

Just then, the bedroom door shook and buckled, as whatever was on the other side, threw itself at their bedroom door.

Both girls screamed, and Ellie jumped on the bed.

*Bam!*

Again, all its weight was thrown against the door, trying to break it down. Ellie threw the covers over her head, just barely stifling her second scream. Quickly Sammie swung the chair around, backed it up against the door, and pulled on the wheel brake.

There was more scratching and then a low, threatening howl, that grew in intensity.

"A wolf, Ellie, It's a wolf."

Ellie peered from under the covers at Sammie in the wheelchair attempting to hold back the hungry animal. The wolf, determined, again threw himself against the door, pushing the chair forward a fraction of an inch.

"Ellie, I can't hold this by myself. We need something heavy. She looked around the room. "The dresser!"

Ellie jumped from the bed, ran to the dresser and pushed with all her strength, but only succeeded in moving it partway.

"Sammie, I can't do it myself. It's too heavy." Tears of frustration rolled down her cheeks.

The wolf went back to scratching, and then the sound changed. Sammie looked down and saw the animal's paw under the door. Thinking quickly, she rolled her heavy wheelchair over it. With a loud cry from the animal, the paw disappeared, and she heard a painful whimper. She knew she had but a few precious seconds.

"Quick, now!"

Sammie rolled over to help Ellie with the dresser. Between the two of them, they managed to push it in front of the door. No sooner then they had when the wolf threw itself against the door.

"Go away. Git!" the girls shouted together as Sammie wheeled her chair, so it was sideways against the dresser. "Climb in my lap. The extra weight should prevent the door from opening."

Ellie sat on her sister's lap, and they waited in silence, listening. After three more attempts, the wolf also went silent.

"Is it gone?" Ellie whispered.

"I don't know. It might be waiting for us to come out."

Half an hour passed without a sound. Yawning, Ellie wrapped her arms around her sister's neck and laid her head on Sammie's shoulder. Within minutes she was asleep.

Their physical closeness helped soothe some of the aching loneliness Sammie felt. But, oh, how she wished her parents were there. *Pa would have taken that wolf out immediately. He would never have been caught without his rifle nearby.* She listened for signs of the wolf. Nothing. Had it gone back outside? Then she turned her head, looked at the small window in the room, and shuddered.

# Chapter Ten

## The Morning After

Sammie didn't sleep in the bed that night but fell asleep in her chair. Ellie had found her way to bed sometime in the middle of the night and was in a deep sleep. Early, before the rooster crowed, Sammie cracked open the bedroom door, looking for the wolf. When she didn't see anything, she ventured out into the living area.

"Is it gone yet?" Ellie asked.

Sammie jumped up in her chair. She thought her sister was still asleep.

"Don't scare me like that!"

When the wolf didn't appear, she grew braver and moved further into the room, inspecting the damage.

"Look at this mess," Ellie said, following behind her.

They scanned the chaos and destruction that was once their beautiful home. Overturned furniture, pots, and pans, scattered everywhere, and several of their mother's china cups broken, scattered around the room. Food had been removed from their proper storage, and remnants of the wolf's meal were also evident in the damage.

Sammie sighed, "The dry summer is bringing the animals down from the mountains. They're looking for food just like Pa said they would."

"Well, I wish they would look somewhere else," Ellie said as she started to clean up the mess to help Sammie bring order back to the room.

"That was dangerous last night," Sammie said as she fried up some of their dwindling supply of smoked bacon and eggs. "Way too dangerous for my liking."

As they sat at the table to eat breakfast, both girls were still feeling a bit tense, especially whenever they glanced at the broken front window.

"The first thing we need to do is board up that window," Sammie said as she forked the last bite of eggs into her mouth.

"There's wood in the barn and nails."

Once the girls had finished eating and cleaning, they measured the damaged window. After that, Sammy grabbed her rifle, and the girls headed for the barn. Along one wall, Ellie found a pile of boards their Pa had cut to replace some of the wood fencings around the pasture.

"Everything is just too big or too small," Ellie complained, "Like these fence boards." Sammie leaned forward and examined one of the boards.

"They'll work. We'll cut 'em to fit."

It took longer than they wanted to saw the boards in half because neither had used a saw before. Thanks to Pa, Sammie had some experience with a hammer and nails. Once they finished cutting the boards, it took them several trips to haul the planks to the cabin. Sammie boarded up the lower part of the window as far as she could reach. While Ellie fetched a four-legged stool to do the upper portions, when it was done, the girls stepped back to inspect their handiwork.

"It doesn't look right," Ellie commented, eyeing some of the bent nails that still stuck out of the wooden planks.

"We did a good job together," Sammie replied.

"Yes, *we* did," Ellie laughed, "Even if it is cockeyed."

"Ellie, can you fetch some water from the well? We used most of what we had inside for cleaning up breakfast."

Ellie smiled, saluted her sister with a teasing, "Aye, aye, Capi-tan!" Grabbed the bucket and headed across the farmyard to the well, marching, knees high, to her music. She was beginning to understand that working as a team made the day go much smoother. Her smile widened. The air was fresh for a change, and the scent of her mother's flowers along the porch, especially the sweet peas, filled her nostrils.

Inside the cabin, Sammie rolled over to the fire and stirred the embers, throwing on two more logs to build it up. Wheeling back to the kitchen, she filled a pot with the remaining water and set it on the stove. *Bean soup and cornbread should taste good tonight for supper,* she thought.

Moments later, she heard footsteps on the front porch. The door swung open, and Ellie struggled inside with the heavy bucket of water.

"Thank you. Pour it in there," Sammie pointed to a large pot sitting next to the sink.

"Sammie, I'm going to bring in some logs from the woodpile."

"Remember to keep an eye out. I'm not sure where that wolf went. Should you see a movement of any kind, get back here immediately."

Sammie threw a handful of beans into the soup pot and began chopping vegetables.

Minutes later, the door flew open, and Ellie ran in wide-eyed and out of breath.

"The Indian, he's watching...from the woods!"

"What?"

"*The* Indian. I *saw* him...all of him! He...he's tall, big...huge! Like eight feet!"

50

Sammie grabbed her rifle and rolled onto the porch. She scanned the hillside as she rolled down the wooden ramp into the yard and headed toward the scattered pile of firewood Ellie had dropped.

Sammie looked again, but only saw beautiful tall pines and silent forests.

"I can't see him now, but I can feel his eyes," Ellie whispered as she stood beside her sister. "He's here."

Sammie squinted, her eyes slowly searching the mountainside. Nothing.

"Are you sure you saw something."

"Yes. Yes! A thousand times, yes!"

Sammie again looked, but nothing. "I think we should get back to the cabin. Why don't you put the firewood on my lap, so you don't have to carry it?"

Ellie stacked the wood on Sammie's lap and started pushing her toward the cabin.

"I did see him, ya know."

"I believe you, Ellie."

"You do?"

"Yes."

Ellie sighed, "Thank you."

Ellie pushed the wheelchair while glancing back over her shoulder. Still looking for the Indian, she didn't see a rock in the ground ahead of them. When she hit it, the wheelchair tilted to one side, spilling Sammie and the firewood to the ground.

"There he is!" Ellie screamed into her sister's ear.

Sammie lay on the ground, the rifle thrown beyond her reach. The wheelchair was on its side, the top wheel still spinning madly, and the firewood lay scattered on the ground.

"I'm sorry. I'm sorry," Ellie apologized, feeling terrible.

Ellie quickly reached for the rifle and gave it to her sister. Sammie pointed the gun toward the trees, looking through the gun sight. Not seeing anything, the two girls struggled to the right the wheelchair, all the while looking toward the hills. Sammie pulled herself up into the chair without a word. If the Indian was watching, he now knew they were weak and alone.

"Leave the firewood, Ellie, and let's get back to the cabin."

There was no argument. Without a word, she pushed her sister across the yard.

Sammie decided the rest of the chores would have to go undone. Their safety was more important. Back in the cabin, both girls felt an unfamiliar, overwhelming fear. Not knowing what to do, they went over everything their father had told them. They realized it wasn't much, and certainly didn't cover this situation. That night as they lay in bed side by side, they both kept checking the small bedroom window, Ellie wanted nothing more than to be in New York, and Sammie wanted nothing more than to be out of her wheelchair.

# Chapter Eleven

## Independence

As Ben made another turn toward town and away from the mountains, he spotted a covered wagon ahead, pulled over to the side of the road. It looked like they were headed in the other direction. He slowed down just as a young man stepped from behind the back of the wagon and waved frantically at him. Then an older man joined him, wiping his hands on his britches.

"Howdy," the younger man called out, a frown creasing his forehead.

"Howdy," Ben replied as he eased to a stop.

A woman and a small boy poked their heads out of the front of the little wagon. Then another boy, about twelve, joined his father.

"We're having some trouble here," the older man told him. "Got waylaid back aways, and we're running three days behind. Almost out of water and food, too. Have you any you can spare, neighbor?"

"I...we do have some. I'm willing to share what I can," Ben replied.

Ben climbed over the seat and into the back of the wagon. Although he had rigged a blanket to shelter her from the direct sunlight, Ellen was still warm, sweating, and unconscious, but her breathing was steady. He wiped her forehead with a wet cloth, then looked at the provisions he had packed. Thinking of the family, he pulled a good portion, enough for them to get by for three days, and took one of the two small barrels of water he'd brought.

Just then, the older man poked his head over the back of the wagon, startling Ben.

"Wife sick?" he asked, nodding at Ellen.

"She's been hurt," he said quietly. "Taking her to the doctor in Independence. It's been rough on her. The pain is bad, so she's passed out most of the time."

Ben selected a few bundles of food and started handing them to the man, who smiled at him and nodded. His eldest son took the food from his pa's hands and disappeared.

"I can give you one of these water barrels, and I think that'll last you the three days." He bent down to pull out one of the barrels, watching Ellen as he worked.

"Yeah, but we can't be too sure, so I'll take both those water barrels, and the rest of the food, neighbor."

Ben looked up, confused. The man grinned back, pointing a two-barrel shotgun right into Ben's face. "All of it."

"But my wife, she has to have water, food. I'll give you my portion."

"You will give me every drop of water and every bit of food in that wagon. I've got a family to feed." He jabbed Ben with the end of the shotgun, as he surveyed the unconscious woman. "She looks to be in a bad way. She probably won't live much longer anyway, and I got to take care of my family first. I won't take your horses, so you can try to get to Independence. Best, be careful, though. Independence sits close to 11,000 feet on Independence Pass. It's a steep, nail-biting passage, especially for those traveling in a wagon."

Ben could see through the front of their wagon, and he watched the two boys guzzling down the small supply of water. Without a word, he handed over the second barrel of water and pushed the remaining food toward the man. There was still a canteen with water under the front seat, and Benjamin managed to shove a small packet of dried fruit under a blanket. He just wanted the man to leave so that they could get on their way, now more than ever.

Backing away, the man scowled and lowered his gun. "I'm not a bad man, but I gotta take care of my own. Go on, get outta here. I hope your wife gets better."

Climbing back into the back seat, Ben clicked his tongue at the horses and pulled out, berating himself the whole time. *If I hadn't stopped, we'd still have our food and water. Now what? I'll have to go faster and look for water.*

**\*\*\*\***

The man who had robbed him wasn't kidding when he described the road leading to Independence. Ben was glad his wife was unconscious. While she wasn't exactly afraid of heights, she would have found this passage too much to handle. The road was barely wide enough for the wagon, leaving only a foot of space on each side of the wheels. Even the horses were nervous. The left side was solid rock, part of the mountain. The right was a sheer drop-off, also making him a little queasy. He kept his eyes solidly fixed on the road ahead.

When the road finally leveled off and spread out to a broader space, Ben sighed with relief, trying not to think about the trip back. They didn't have to travel too much further, and before long, they approached a graveyard just outside the town where two men were digging a fresh grave.

"I wonder who died?" He said aloud, even though his wife was still unconscious.

As they entered the town, he was surprised that not that many people seemed to be around. It was a mining town, by the look of things. He noticed one or two boarded-up storefronts. That was a bad sign like the place was on its way to becoming a ghost town. Ben decided to stop by the sheriff's office to ask about the doctor as he slowed down to a stop as a man stepped outside from the saloon across the street.

"Pardon me, sir," Ben asked. "Can you tell me where I can find the doctor?"

"His office is down that away on the right. But he ain't there…'xactly."

Ben figured that even if the doctor wasn't in, he'd have to come back eventually, so he pushed the horses just a few more yards down the street. As he pulled up, he discovered a small crowd of people gathered in the doctor's front room. Hopping down from the wagon, he was about to step up onto the porch when the door opened.

Ignoring the people lingering there, he walked right through the middle of the townspeople gathered in the front room and came to a sudden halt. Instead of the doctor, he discovered a casket. With some confusion, he watched four pallbearers lift and carried the coffin, a plain wooden pine box, through the room and out the front door. The people filed out after it. Not wanting to wait another moment, Ben grabbed the last man in line – a rather well-dressed man with a large head.

"I need to see the doctor right away. It's critical. Please, where's the doctor?"

Without a word, the man, who just happened to be the town sheriff, turned and pointed to the casket. "He's dead. Liked the bottle a bit too much, and it finally rotted out his gut."

Ben turned pale.

"Then, where do people go when they need medical treatment? Does he have a replacement?"

The man shook his head. "Just the vet, almost as good as the doc, in my opinion."

The Sheriff re-joined the procession, leaving Ben flabbergasted. "A vet? I can't take my wife to a veterinarian. He'd…he'd probably put her down!

No one paid any attention to Ben, and he began to panic. Feeling utterly helpless, he turned this way and that, looking for what, he didn't know. Then he spotted a poster fastened to the front door of the deceased doctor's office:

*GOT TROUBLE WITH YOUR BACK?*

*What miner doesn't?*

*Well, you're in luck!*

*July 5 – 11*

*Dr. Edward Feldman,*

*a renowned back specialist from Boston, Massachusetts*

*will be right here in Independence.*

*Do not delay. Schedule your appointment NOW.*

*The doctor will be here for only seven days, and he can*

*See only so many patients during that time.*

*Don't miss this chance to see a real specialist.*

Ben pulled the poster off the door and ran toward the Sheriff. When he caught up with him, he held the sign up and asked, "This doctor, this specialist, where is he today?"

The Sheriff shook his head and pointed to a woman in the line ahead. "Ask the doc's nurse. She would know as she's been making the appointments."

Glancing at the wagon, Ben ran up to the sobbing woman, turned to face her, and removed his hat. "I'm so sorry to hear about the good doctor's death, but could you help me? Please?" He held up the poster. "This doctor, the specialist, where is he now? Where can I find him?"

The woman looked up and saw the desperate look on his face, dried her tears, and responded kindly despite her grief. "He's in Aspen, about thirty miles east from here. He'll be there for two weeks."

Ben gave her a slight bow and took her hand in his. "Thank you, kind lady, thank you."

"He'll be coming here directly from Aspen."

"I can't wait. My wife…she fell from the hayloft, and I think she broke her back. She's in a powerful lot of pain and needs to see him as soon as possible."

She looked into his worried eyes and saw his desperation. "I'm so sorry to hear that. I hope he can help."

\*\*\*\*

Ben looked at the sky. Judging from the sun's position, it was mid-afternoon. Thanking the nurse, he crossed to the wagon to check on Ellen. Using a few drops of water from the canteen, he wiped her brow and face to try and cool her off.

Her eyes blinked open, and he smiled at her and lifted her head enough to give her a drink sip of the precious water.

"I know this water is tepid at best, sweetheart, but we're in Independence now, so I'll stock up on freshwater and supplies." He lovingly pushed the damp hair back off her face and softly kissed her parched lips.

"Poor Ben, this is such a burden for you," Ellen said quietly.

His expression momentarily grew fierce, then gentled again. "No, my love, this is

58

not a burden. *You* are not a burden. Don't ever think that. I love you, and I will do whatever it takes to get you well again."

She reached out, took his hand, and smiled weakly. "I know. I know you will. Have you talked to the doctor yet?"

Ben's face fell. "I'm sorry, Ellen, the doctor here passed away yesterday. They were taking him out to be buried when we arrived."

"What...?"

"Shh, it's alright. We're in luck. A back specialist is in Aspen right now, Ellen! He'll be there for two weeks. A real back specialist, from Boston! It means another thirty-mile trek, but the nurse here says he's an excellent doctor." *At least I hope he is.*

"But what if we miss him? Thirty miles is a long way."

"If that happens, then we'll meet him on the way. I just don't want to wait two weeks in this town. We won't miss him, I promise."

She nodded and closed her eyes.

"Are you hungry? I can get us some home cooking at the café here."

"Mm, that sounds heavenly," Ellen said with a smile. "It seems forever since I've eaten anything but trail food."

"I'll pull the wagon over and see what they've got."

Ben climbed over the seat and gently eased the wagon past a couple of buildings. After pulling to a stop, he spotted a sign in the window advertising rooms for rent above the eatery. He looked up at the second and third floors with longing. It would be so beautiful to sleep in a soft bed for the night, but he couldn't carry Ellen and the makeshift stretcher himself. And he didn't want to put her through any additional pain.

Stepping down from the wagon, he glanced back at his wife. "I'll be back soon with some real food."

"Ben," she called softly, "Why don't you rent a room for the night? You could use a good night's rest for a chance. I'll be fine here in the wagon." Ben's heart swelled with love at the unselfishness of his wife. In all of her pain, she was thinking of his comfort. He could not lose her. He wouldn't want to live without her.

"No. I won't leave you alone out here all night in a strange town."

"But, Ben…"

He stuck his head back in the wagon. "As pretty as you are, someone might run away with you!" he teased. "Now, you stay put – no dancin' till I get back with some hot food."

A middle-aged woman, kind of thick around the middle, had stepped out of the restaurant and overheard their conversation. She walked over to the side of the wagon and peeked inside. Ben turned to her, but before he could say a word, she spoke.

"Howdy," she said, sticking out her hand, which he shook. "I'm Fran. This here's my place." She pointed to the sign in a large front window that said, *Fran's Good Eats and Rooms for Rent.*

"Ben. And this is my wife, Ellen."

"Glad to meet ya both. You sick, Ma'am?"

"No," Ben replied for his wife. "She fell from our hayloft and broke her back."

Fran shook her head. "I'm mighty sorry to hear that. Lucky for you, a specialist is comin' here in a couple weeks. Maybe he can fix you up. In the meantime, why don't you stay in one of my rooms? It'll be a lot more comfortable than this here wagon. I'll even give ya'll a discounted rate, since you'll be here a spell."

"That's mighty nice of you, Fran, but I need to get her to the doctor as soon as possible."

"Surely then you'll want to spend the night, both of you get a decent night's rest, and leave first thing in the morning. I'll tell you what. Pay for your meals, and I'll throw in the room for free. The food is good if I do say so myself," she laughed and patted her stomach.

"That sure sounds tempting, but Ellen has to stay on this board, and I can't carry her myself without causing her more pain."

Fran asked. "Got plenty of willing hands to help. Even if she has to stay on that there board, she can have a soft pillow for her head, a crisp, clean sheet to cover her, and a good meal in private. We get a decent breeze in some of the rooms, and I know just the one to put you in. What do you say?"

"Yes," Ellen said, overriding her husband, who was about to refuse. "It would be nice to get out of the sun and heat, even if it's only until morning."

"But the pain…"

"Don't you worry none. Once the funeral's over, I'll send my son over to the nurse to get some laudanum."

"Then it's settled, thank you, Fran," Ellen said, giving her husband a firm look.

Once Ellen received a dose of pain medicine, several men volunteered to carry her upstairs. Amazingly, they were able to do so without causing her too much discomfort. They laid her and the board on one side of the bed.

"Hope you get to feeling better, ma'am," they said with a respectful nod. Fran tucked a pillow under her head and pulled up the sheet to cover her. "If you like, I come up after supper and give you a wash and get you into some clean clothes."

"Oh, I can't think of anything better! That would be wonderful," Ellen said with a sigh.

"Now, I'll bet you're hungry." She looked at Ben. "Why don't you come downstairs and we'll rustle up something for you and your missus to eat. Supper won't be ready for a few hours yet."

That evening after supper, Fran came back to the room with everything she would need to do the job. "Why don't you go on over to the saloon and relax, Ben, while Ellen and I get her cleaned up and comfortable. Don't you worry, I'll be as careful with her as a newborn baby. Go on."

"Well, I…."

"Go ahead, Ben," his wife urged. "Fran and I will be just fine here."

Knowing that if he stayed, it would embarrass his wife to have him there while another woman bathed her, he nodded and left. Spotting a bathhouse just a couple doors down, Ben decided to make use of it. For fifteen cents, he could have a warm bath himself. He thought it might be pleasant after all the dusty days spent on the road. For two more dollars, he could get fresh undergarments and a clean shirt. He thought Ellen would appreciate that.

After his bath, he saw the sheriff who gave him the right directions for the quickest route to Aspen. It seemed like the road wouldn't cause too much additional discomfort for Ellen.

Ben walked over to the general store for supplies. He was standing at the counter when a large man in dirty clothes and scuffed boots limped in.

"How's the trapping going, Dugger," the storekeeper asked.

"Bout the same as usual," the trapper replied.

The trapper turned and looked at Ben. "Don't recall seeing you here before, friend. You new in town?"

"Just passing through," Ben replied, glancing Dugger's way.

"Say, is that your wagon down in front of Fran's?"

"It is."

"Where ya headin'?"

"Aspen. My wife needs to see the doctor there. She was injured in an accident."

"Sorry to hear that. Hope the doc there can fix her up good," Dugger said.

"Thank you. He's a visiting back specialist. If my wife has any chance of getting better, hopefully, he'll be the man to do it."

Dugger nodded. "Specialist, huh? Them specialists usually cost a lot of money, or so I hear."

"That's true, but I'll give him whatever he wants, as long as he can fix my wife's back," Ben said earnestly.

His reply got Dugger to wonder if Ben was carrying around a lot of money. *If he is, I could put it to a lot better use than giving it to some fancy doctor.* "Not many folks could afford to do that."

"I don't have a lot of money. Use to back in New York. I got tired of the big city, so I became a farmer a few years back. Sunk most of what I had into the land." Ben wasn't about to tell him about the money in the New York bank and stock exchange.

Dugger thought about the pair of horses hitched to the farmer's wagon. If he had them, he'd use one for riding and one to carry his furs and gear. "Say, that's a fine pair of horse flesh you got. Interested in selling them? I could offer a fair price that would certainly help pay the medical bills."

Ben shook his head. "They're not for sale."

"I mean, I'd buy them once you got the wife treated and back home again."

"Sorry, I need those horses on the farm. Don't have any spares," Ben told him.

"Staying at Fran's?"

"Yes."

"Maybe I'll see you later over there."

Ben nodded and finished paying his bill.

# Chapter Twelve

## Cowgirl

The next day the girls had no choice. They had to do the farm chores. When Sammie got to the barn, the door was wide open. Unlocking the safety on the rifle in her lap, she entered cautiously and immediately spotted two gruesome piles of blood, feathers, chicken beaks, and feet. Something had killed and eaten two of their chickens. *Maybe it was the wolf or some other beast,* Sammie thought grimly.

Ellie had fallen behind, and when she caught up to Sammie, she asked, "What's wrong? Why have you stop...? Ewwww! Something killed our chickens!"

Leaning forward, they examined the dirt and found a set of tracks leading away from the animal remains.

"How did it get inside the barn?" Ellie asked.

Sammie confronted her sister. "Did you leave the barn door open yesterday?"

"I..." Ellie's hand flew to her mouth. "I...I forgot. Some of the chickens got out, and I left the door open so they could come back inside."

Sammie closed her eyes, fighting the anger that filled her, but failing. "Don't *ever* do that again!"

"But how were they supposed to get back inside? If I had closed the door, they would have gotten eaten anyway," Ellie insisted.

"You catch them or round them up and put them back in the coop. You *know* better than that, Ellie."

"I'm sorry. I'm sorry." Feeling horrible that she'd disappointed her sister again,

65

Ellie turned and ran back to the cabin. She was trying, but there was so much to remember and too many chores. When would ma and pa be back, she desperately needed them to come home.

Sammie turned with a sigh, feeling bad about yelling at Ellie. She needed her sister to help but wasn't sure how much she could expect from a twelve-year-old. Right now, she had to milk the cows, Daisy and Annabel. Sammie also needed to check on Annabel, as the young cow was due to give birth any day.

As she pushed herself up to the stall, she saw Annabel lying on her side. The slow breathing told Sammie that the cow was in labor and had been struggling to give birth, probably all night. That was too long. The calf inside her must be a breach, thought Sammie. A calf was breach when its back end was near the opening, and unable to come out. In that position, it was trapped. A calf typically was born front feet first, then the head, followed by the rest of the body. The baby calf would die inside, and the mother soon after if the calf was still breached.

Sammie knew she had to get the little calf out quickly.

"Ellie! I need your help."

Sammie looked at the barn door, hoping to see her sister running in.

"Ellie, I need your help!" she yelled louder.

Sammie watched the door, but no sister was coming to help.

Annabel bellowed in pain.

Sammie rolled over to the back wall of the barn and grabbed a rope and a pulley and placed them in her lap. Wasting no time, she returned to Annabel's side, slid from her wheelchair and sat alongside the struggling, and now distressed, mother. Carefully, she reached inside the cow and tied the rope around the baby's back legs. She knew she couldn't turn the calf around; it was too large. This was probably the only way to save the little calf. She inserted the other end of the rope through the pulley to gain some leverage. Then, she pulled on the line, trying to drag the baby calf out of its mother.

Sammie pulled and pulled, her muscles straining. Nothing moved. Without the use of her legs, she had to use her upper body strength to pull the rope. It was the only thing she could think of to save the calf and Annabel. She pulled with all her might. Still no movement, but she wouldn't give up and continued to tug as sweat ran down her face.

"Ellie!" she screamed.

Sammie looked once again toward the door of the barn, still no sister.

Taking a deep breath, she pulled again, but the calf did not move, not even an inch. She didn't want anything to die today, especially not today. With a considerable effort, which pulled her whole body right out of the chair, she gave it a good yank.

Suddenly there was movement, and she saw the calf's back hooves. With new hope, she pulled the rope again, just as hard. Now she could see the hind legs. Her arms shaking with fatigue, Sammie knew she could not stop pulling, even with the cow's discomfort. Half of the baby was now outside. Grasping the rope with new determination, she felt her palms blister, but she pulled again, and again until the baby was completely out. Sammie quickly slid back to the newborn and wiped the mucous and blood away from the calf's nose. Now that the little face was free of liquids, the baby took its first breath.

Smiling at the little calf, Sammie untied the rope from its back legs. With large brown eyes, the calf studied her face, seeming to understand what Sammie had done to save its life. The calf licked her face, and Sammie started to cry.

The calf slowly, deliberately, stood up and wobbled around the stall. Annabel watched her baby and then rose to her feet so that the baby could nurse.

*Life is wonderful,* Sammie thought. Exhausted, but filled with joy, she laid back on the hay. Every muscle in her upper body was sore. *There will be no death today*, she thought. *Not today.*

Regaining her strength, she first went to the water pump to wash off the birthing fluid and blood from her arms; then, she started toward the house to see what her sister was doing. When Sammie entered the cabin, she saw her sister sitting on the couch, reading *David Copperfield*, one of her favorite books.

"What are you doing?"

"What does it look like I'm doing?"

"Didn't you hear me yelling for you?"

"Once, but when you didn't yell again, I thought you really didn't need me."

"When I call you, I need you to come immediately. Do you hear me?"

"Yes, I hear you."

"Then, put down the book."

Ellie slammed the book shut.

"There. Now, what did you want?" Ellie asked, noticing for the first time her sister's wet clothes and how dirty and disheveled she looked.

"I can't believe you. You sit here reading when you know there are a hundred tasks to do on the farm."

"Your farm, you're the one who loves it here. I'm a city girl, a *New York City* girl! What did you need me for anyway?" she whined as she looked up from the chair, crossing her arms.

"Annabel had her calf."

"She did! Oh, I have to go see." She jumped up and headed for the door, then turned around, realizing how tired Sammie looked, and how difficult it must have been to deliver the calf by herself.

"I'm sorry. What else is there to do?

Sammie was not only tired but angry. She felt as if she was doing everything by herself, overwhelmed and upset, she hit Ellie with the blunt truth.

"Collect the vegetables and can them for winter, bring in firewood for the stove, clean the cabin, cut hay in the field, feed the chickens, horses, and pigs, do the laundry, and fix the fence the goats destroyed, to name just a few."

Ellie blinked. That was a lot. But she knew she'd let her sister down and wanted to make up for it. "I can start on that while you finish cleaning up. You stink."

# Chapter Thirteen

## Dugger

While Ben loaded up the wagon, Dugger looked through an open doorway and saw Fran gently securing a woman to a wooden board. It wasn't hard to figure out who she was. He stepped inside the room, set down a bundle of furs, and doffed his hat.

"Mornin' ladies, don't mean to seem nosy," He turned to Ellen, "but I think I talked to your husband last night at the general store."

"You must be the trapper Ben told me about," Ellen said with a smile.

Dugger looked like a new man today. Between his bath the night before and donning clean clothes, he was reasonably presentable.

Sizing him up, Ellen thought to herself, *Well, he's probably been on the trail for several days. What did Ben expect when he described the man as grubby? We weren't so beautiful looking ourselves before we cleaned up.*

"Bet you'll be happy to get this doctor business over with and head back home," Dugger said, fishing for information.

"Oh my, yes. I've been so worried. We had to leave our daughters behind. The eldest is a grown woman, but the youngest is only twelve…no. She just had a birthday a few days ago, so she's thirteen. Never been on their own before, but I'm sure Samantha is handling things just fine. She's a very clever girl."

Dugger didn't show it, but what she said caught his interest. *Two girls all alone? I wonder what there is there worth stealing.* Aloud he said, "I understand your concern, Missus. You live far from here?"

"It's a fair piece, especially traveling slowly by wagon. Ben said we had to travel up Independence Pass." She sighed. "He said it was a good thing I was asleep because it's a terrifying trip."

"Yes, I have traveled it quite a bit myself, but of course, I wasn't in a wagon. Going by horse or on foot isn't as bad." He stopped and pretended to be thinking about something. Then nodding, he looked at her. "You know, I'll be trapping out that way. I could stop and check in on your girls for you. Tell them I saw ya and all."

"Thank you so much, that's very kind of you. But we'll be returning home in just a few days."

"Just thought I'd offer. Might ease the children's minds a bit to know you made it to town and goin' on to Aspen. 'Specially since I hear them Comanches are getting' a bit restless again. Seems like them no good injuns aren't happy if they ain't stirrin' up trouble now and again."

Ellen looked worried. "Well, maybe…."

Before she could finish her sentence, Ben walked in with three men.

"We're ready to get you loaded up, Ellen." He spotted Dugger and nodded. "Is there something you need?"

"No, no indeed. Just walkin' past on my way out and noticed the open door. Thought I'd stop by and say hello to the missus." He leaned over and picked up his bundle of furs.

"We're just leaving, too." Ben's look spoke volumes. He wanted the trapper gone.

"Well, good luck to ya both." Dugger tipped his hat again and was about to leave when Ellen spotted a sliver of red fur in his bundle.

71

"Wait." She looked up at Ben. "Please?"

Ben looked at her curiously.

"Is that fox fur I see in your bundle?" She asked Dugger.

"Yes, ma'am, it is. Would you like to see it?"

Ellen looked at Ben, her head nodding yes.

Ben could not refuse his wife, especially now. "We would," he said, turning to Dugger.

The trapper dug it out. It was the most beautiful red fur.

"May I see it closer?" Ellen asked.

Dugger brought it over and handed it to her. She ran her hands down the luxurious, soft fur and rubbed it against her cheek. "This would be so pretty on a dress for Ellie." She looked up at Ben. "For when she goes back to New York. She's going to be an actress," she explained to the trapper.

"What about Sammie?" Ben asked.

"Oh, Sammie would never wear fur. She loves animals far too much. We can find something nice to buy for her in the next town."

"How much?" Ben asked the trapper.

"Well, let's see. It's a fine quality pelt. I could sell it for $10.00."

"That's a lot of money," Ben said. He turned toward his wife. "We don't know how much we're going to need for the doctor to fix you up."

"That's true," Ellen said thoughtfully. She turned to Dugger. "You said you would be trapping in our area for a while. Right?"

"That's right."

"Can you hold onto it for me? Once we get back home, I have some money set aside. When you're close by, you could stop and sell it to me then, right?"

"Well, I suppose so. 'Course I'd need to know how to find ya."

Forgetting her earlier caution, Ellen told him of the farm. She just had to have that fox for Ellie.

Dugger put the pelt back in his bundle and stood up straight. "Then I guess I'll be seeing you later."

"You promise to keep it for me?"

"Yes, ma'am, I surely will." He nodded as he walked out the door and mounted his horse. He was gone in a minute. Little did Ellen realize what she had just unleashed on her daughters.

Four of Fran's male guests took Ellen downstairs and settled her into the wagon. She thanked them for their help, and as they left to go about their business, Fran came over with a basket filled with goodies.

"There are fresh biscuits in here along with some fruit tarts and a few things you don't normally get to eat on the road."

"Oh, we couldn't possibly…." Ben began.

"No, I insist. You and your wife are good people, and I want to do this for you. It's not much, but it might make the trip ahead of a little nicer," Fran insisted.

Ellen reached out, and Fran took her hand. "You've been so kind to us. God bless you."

"He does every day…every day."

****

Two days later, a very tired Sammie sat on the porch. Not getting enough sleep was taking a toll on her. Since all seemed in good order, she thought it would be alright to take a quick nap.

When she opened her eyes, she saw the wolf racing toward her.

Sammie brought her rifle up to aim, but the wolf was closing in. Fast. She aimed the gun at the animal, her hands shaking. But she knew she was out of time.

# Chapter Fourteen

## Trouble for Two

Suddenly, a shot rang out behind her, and the wolf dropped in its tracks.

Sammie couldn't believe her eyes. "Ellie, what a shot!" she said as she turned her wheelchair around.

"What happened?" Ellie asked as she ran from the kitchen to the porch. One look at her sister's expression made her turn to stare at the trapper coming out of the woods. He walked with a limp.

A man in his mid-forties, dressed in buckskin pants held up with wide red suspenders, a worn, dirty dark green woven shirt, and scuffed boots approached. He smiled at them, holding his rifle high in the air. Rugged and robust, he had a thick head of dark hair and a beard with bits of grey. His skin was tanned and leathery from constant exposure to the sun.

"You all right? You must be Miss Samantha. The name's Dugger."

The girls exchanged glances. They were warned to beware of strangers, especially trappers and hunters, but this one had just saved Sammie's life. Realizing they were suspicious, Dugger stopped about ten feet away.

"How do you know my name?" Sammie asked, slowly raising her rifle.

Dugger smiled. It was a friendly smile, but a gold front tooth gleaming in the sunlight, spoiled it a bit.

"On my way to the valley, I met your ma and pa in Independence. They had to go on to another town to find a doctor. The trip was goin' slower than they figured. They were worried about you two bein' alone. Asked me to stop by and make sure you were doin' alright if I found myself nearby." He spoke quietly, reassuringly. "Looks like I got here just in time."

"You saw our Ma and Pa on the trail?" Ellie asked excitedly. "How was Ma?"

"She was in a lot of pain. They couldn't land a break. Your pa was takin' her to the next town, to a specialist. They'll be two, three more weeks gone, I 'spect."

"I want to thank you for shooting that wolf," Sammie said, wanting to change the subject for her sister's sake. "I'm afraid it got the drop on me. I wasn't quick enough."

"Well now, that could happen to anyone, Miss," Dugger said.

Sammie noticed the ragged scar on his left temple, running from his hairline to his eye.

"I see you have a limp," Sammie said. "Are you hurt?"

Dugger shook his head. "No, it's an old injury I got as a youngster. The local doctor fixed me up good, but it still pains me, especially when the weather changes."

While he talked, Sammie looked at the stuff the man had draped about his person. It was typical trapper stuff: a large pack, probably with a couple of animal skins and some salted meat, a revolver in a holster, a large hunting knife, and a rifle now slung over his shoulder. He also carried a smaller embroidered bag that made her curious as to what was inside. It wasn't the sort of thing one usually saw a trapper carry.

By now, Dugger stood next to the porch.

"Say, I'm right, thirsty. Need to fill my canteen, too."

"There's a pump near the barn. Help yourself," Sammie told him.

"Thank ya kindly," the trapper said as he walked past the dead wolf and headed for the pump. "Got to be going. Best of luck to ya."

As soon as he was gone, Ellie came back out on the porch.

"It sounds like Ma and Pa won't be back anytime soon."

"Pa will get back as soon as he can," Sammie said to encourage her sister. "And we know they reached Independence, and ma is still, well, she's fine. And Pa will get her to that doctor. If this trapper's right, it's a specialist."

She decided to bring more wood up to the cabin, but halfway to the barn, she felt as though she was being watched. Turning her head, she saw the Indian standing high on the mountainside.

She screamed. "Dugger, Mr. Dugger, come back!"

The old trapper was too far away to hear her, and the Indian, hearing her call the trapper, darted back into the trees. A few minutes later, he emerged again, closer this time. He smiled shyly and held up his hand in greeting Sammie, who panicked and wheeled as fast as she could back into the cabin.

\*\*\*\*

The sun was just beginning to peek over the mountains when Sammie awoke, still sitting by the window. Rubbing her tired eyes, she was mad at herself for falling asleep with an Indian somewhere nearby. She had meant to stay awake the whole night to keep watch. Her rifle still lay across her lap.

After breakfast, Sammie rolled out onto the porch looking in every direction. As she turned her chair to go back inside, she noticed a neatly stacked pile of firewood by the door. Her mouth fell open, and her eyes searched the hillside.

"Ellie, did you stack the firewood?"

"No." Ellie joined her on the porch.

Sammie looked across the field toward the trees.

"I think the Indian stacked our wood," Sammie said.

"Why would an Indian do that?"

"I honestly don't know."

# Chapter Fifteen

## On the Road Again

The trip to Aspen would take two to three days, depending on the condition of the roads they were traveling and how fast Ben dared to go without causing his wife too much pain. Under normal circumstances, a wagon could cover the distance in a little over a day, but because of the necessity of going slow, it would take longer. It had taken more time than he'd planned to load the supplies, and he hadn't had the heart to wake Ellen too early, so they got a late start.

The sun was low in the sky when Ben found a good spot to camp for the night. He wanted enough daylight to look for firewood and make supper before it got too dark. Thanks to Fran's generosity, their meals weren't quite so dull. One day they got lucky when Ben spotted a rabbit near their camp, which he shot with plans to roast over the fire.

His wife was awake when they stopped for the night.

"How are you feeling," Ben asked her. "Do you need some laudanum?"

"Maybe after we eat. It will help me sleep tonight. For now, why don't you drawback my little roof," she suggested, smiling, "so I can feel some of the cooler evening air."

"One roof removal coming up," Ben joked as he pulled back the blanket he used to shelter her from the sun. He was relieved to find her in good spirits. The extra laudanum they had purchased in Independence had been a Godsend as theirs had run out. It would last them till they reached Aspen, and possibly until they arrived back home. He hoped the specialist would be able to do something else to relieve his wife's pain. He knew that once home, she would refuse to take the drug unless it was necessary. She wouldn't want to become dependent upon it. After cleaning the rabbit, he tied it high up on a branch, to keep it out of the reach of bears and other meat-eating animals. Then he walked over to the side of the wagon and looked in on his wife. "I need to gather some wood for a campfire. I won't stray too far from camp, so if you need anything, just give me a holler."

"I'll be fine, Ben, but do try to hurry." She grinned at him. "My tummy is rumbling something fierce."

He laughed. "Why don't you eat one of the biscuits or a tart to keep you until the rabbit is ready to eat?"

"Good idea."

The basket had been placed next to her so she could reach inside and help herself whenever she was hungry. To save time, Ben ate while they traveled.

Breaking up a few branches close to the camp, Ben started the fire so that when he returned with more wood, they wouldn't have as long to wait until it was hot enough to cook the meat.

Ellen listened to his work until he left to find more wood. A cool mountain breeze blew across the wagon. It felt so excellent after the long hot day that she closed her eyes and listened to the birds and crickets that had begun their evening songs. The sound was like a lullaby, and it sang her to sleep. She had no idea how long she had dozed off when the breaking of a twig woke her.

"Ben?" she asked sleepily, thinking he had returned.

Another snap and the sound of someone moving about brought her completely awake.

"Ben? Is that you?" Her voice was barely above a whisper as fear took hold of her when he did not respond. She lay there, looking around at what little she could see, other than the sky when she heard something that sounded like a child cooing, followed by a soft grunt.

Bears!

A mother and cubs by the sound of it.

Ellen's eyes went to the rabbit, hanging in plain view. Then she saw the mother, a large black bear, standing on her hind legs grunting as it tried to reach the raw meat.

"Uh, uh, uh," came from her muzzle, a quick repetitive grunt as she stretched and swung her paws. It was just out of reach, but the hungry mother bear was determined. With two cubs to feed, she needed more food than usual to produce milk for them.

Dropping down to all four paws, she ambled over to the massive tree trunk and climbed until she reached the extended branch where the food hung. Her cubs squalled for her below. The branch was thick, but whether it would hold the 150-pound bear was debatable. Over the summer and fall, she would double that weight to take her and the cubs through the long cold winter.

Ellen remained quiet, hoping not to attract attention while the bear stretched, but still couldn't quite reach the food. Then it dawned on Ben's wife that the food in the wagon would be its next target.

*Hurry up, Ben,* she thought. The last thing either of them needed was for her to be mauled or killed by a bear. While she didn't want the mother or cubs harmed, she didn't want to give up all their food supplies yet again.

The bear crept cautiously out onto the branch a few inches and tried once more to reach the rabbit.

*Just a few more inches, keep trying,* Ellen thought.

The mother bear gave one more swing and snatched the rabbit as the branch cracked loudly and broke. She fell slowly to the ground, woofing and chomping in fear. The cubs ran over to her, voicing little squeals of mild distress. Then the adult bear shook her head and tore into the rabbit until she swallowed the last piece. Naturally, she was still hungry.

Standing up on all fours, she sniffed the air and turned toward the wagon.

Ellen froze, except to lower her gaze so that she was following the animal with her eyes. The next thing she saw was the bear's head staring into the wagon. Fear shot through her like a bolt of electricity.

Momma bear smelled the food and the human. The bear was as afraid as Ellen was. She lifted her paw and swatted the floor of the wagon, blowing and snorting, telling Ellen to go away. Living in the wilderness, it was a good idea to know as much as possible about bear behavior. Ben had instructed her and both girls on how to handle a bear situation. She knew that the bear didn't want to fight any more than she did. It was just trying to tell her that Ellen was too close, especially with cubs on the scene. Had she appeared more threatening, it would have been a different story.

Typically, black bears rarely attack unless protecting their cubs. While the human was a threat, Ellen was lying down, which made her appear small. The mama bear did not feel as threatened as it would have had Ellen been able to stand up. And since Ellen couldn't, she did the next best thing.

She looked it directly in the animal's eye and said, "Go away, bear. I don't want to hurt you or your babies, but you need to get away from here before my husband comes back."

The animal's response was to pop its jaws, telling her to go away.

"Leave now, bear!" Ellen stated as she tried to remain calm.

Just then, Ben returned with the firewood. His first inclination was to drop the wood and shoot until he saw the cubs. Benjamin wasn't going to condemn them to death by starvation because he'd killed their mother. And he didn't have the heart to shoot the little cubs. As long as his wife was okay, and he'd heard her talking, so he knew she was unharmed. He would try to get the mother bear to take her cubs and go away. He gently laid down the wood, but his actions were enough to get the animal's attention. She turned and dropped down from the back of the wagon.

The tall human male was a much more significant threat, and she lunged just enough that he knew it was a bluff. Standing as straight as possible to make himself appear even taller, Ben spoke in a calm, appeasing tone. "Get out of here, bear. And take your cubs with you. No one here wants to hurt you."

The mother bear hesitated. Then grunting to her cubs, all three ran off.

"Ellen! Ellen!" Ben called as he ran to the wagon and jumped in back to check her over. He found her shaking.

"I'm alright. I'm fine. The bear didn't hurt me, but I'm afraid she ate our supper."

He looked over at the tree, and that was when he saw the sizeable broken branch on the ground. "What was I thinking? I should never have skinned that rabbit before I fetched the firewood and was here to protect you."

"I'm fine, Ben. The rabbit kept her distracted long enough for you to come to my rescue. And I stood my ground, or I should say I laid on the ground and used my very stern 'mother' voice."

Now Ben started to laugh. "I know that voice, so I understand why that bear took off. I'm thankful you never use it on me," he teased her.

"I'm not your mother, Ben. I'm much more than that!" Ben leaned over and kissed his wife.

"Yes, you are. All the same, I won't make that mistake again. I'll build up the fire. She won't come near it, and then take this food and tie it up in a tree, some distance away."

Ellen looked lovingly at her husband. He was a good man, and this was so hard on him. "Look, we'll feast on these wonderful goodies that Fran gave us. I think she thought there were six of us instead of two. Then yes, you can tie the rest of it up in a distant tree. It's been a challenging day, but tomorrow I'm sure things will be better."

# Chapter Sixteen

## Changes

Sammie stared at the large cast iron sink filled with dirty clothes. She reached over and lifted the pitcher to pour water into the drain. It was empty.

"Ellie, can you go to the well and fetch a bucket of water?"

Ellie didn't move.

"If you get the water right now, I'll wash the clothes, and you can use the time to read," Sammie bargained.

"That's a deal." Ellie coughed and wiped her runny nose before grabbing the water bucket and heading outside.

"Are you getting a cold?" Sammie called after her.

"I'm fine - unless it will get me out of fetching water."

"I don't think so," her sister replied with a smile.

Ellie ran to get the chore done as soon as possible so that she could start reading. As she began to pump, the water came very slowly, and then became cloudy and dirty. She poured the dirty water on the ground and started again. This time the water was even nastier, and after pumping the handle three times, the water stopped altogether.

Her hand rubbed her face as she tried to figure out what was wrong with the pump. She knew one thing: this had never happened before. She pumped again and again. Leaving the empty bucket, she walked back to the house.

"Sammie, the pump is broken."

"What?"

"The first bucket was full of dirty water. So I dumped it. Then when I tried to pump again, I got more dirty water. Then the water just stopped coming out."

Sammie felt her muscles tighten up. "Can't anything be easy?" She rolled her chair to the door. "Let's take a look."

The girls went to the pump, and Ellie looked up at the bright blue sky. It certainly was beautiful and hot, with no sign of rain. Ellie tried once more to get some water while her sister watched.

Nothing.

"What are we going to do without water?" Ellie asked.

"Until we figure this out, we'll have to get the water from the lake."

"That will take forever to walk there and back every day," Ellie whined.

"I know, but we need water to survive, and the only water around is in the lake. And that means the rifle is yours to carry," Sammie said, smiling, knowing her sister had wanted to be in charge of the rifle for a long time.

"Really?"

"Really. Now grab the rifle and go fetch us some water."

Both girls knew this was a big deal, a coming of age sort of thing for Ellie. For her big sister, it meant even more. It meant protection, survival. They were learning to fend for themselves, at least for a while. Ma and Pa would be home soon, and things wouldn't be so hard.

**** 

That night, when Ellie changed into her nightgown, she realized it didn't fit the same way. For the past few weeks, she had noticed changes in her body. But without her mother to explain things, she wasn't sure what to think.

"Sammie, can you help me? I can't get this nightdress on. It's too small. It's choking me," she called from the bedroom.

Sammie rolled into the room and watched her sister struggling to get dressed. She realized, that with the work and problems they had dealt with over the past few days, she hadn't noticed that Ellie was growing up.

"Well, I can see why," she laughed. "It's too small."

Ellie's expression went from frustration to dismay. "Am I getting fat?" She ran over to the mirror and examined herself critically.

Sammie chuckled. "No, not fat, you're just growing up. It happens to all of us girls. In the next two years, you will change a lot." She smiled. "Your feet will get big, and probably your nose."

"My nose will get big?" She turned to look in the mirror again. "It *does* look bigger. Look! This is awful. I'm going to be so ugly." She ran to her sister and knelt in front of her. "How can I become a famous actress in the theater if I have this huge nose?"

"It's just for a little while, then the rest of your body will catch up - and everything will match. Really. Trust me, Ellie, you will be beautiful. I think probably the most beautiful actress ever. It all evens out. Just be patient."

"I can't believe this is happening. What else? Is there anything else?"

"Well, yes, of course. You're becoming a young woman. Your shirts and dresses won't fit at all, because you'll start to get breasts, like mine. Like Ma's."

Ellie looked horrified and put her hands over her chest and looked down. "I haven't thought much about that. Does it hurt?"

"Sometimes, but just a little and it's how…it's how…" Sammie paused, trying to remember how Ma had explained it to her, searching for just the right words. "It's how God created us to be women."

"God? I thought you didn't believe in God, not like Ma."

"Well…some things that God does are…. Well, Ma can explain it better when she gets home." Sammie suddenly pointed to Ellie's feet. "I'll bet your shoes are starting to get tight, too."

"Ohhh, they are! I didn't want to tell you. I had such a hard time getting them on this morning. What am I going to do? Did this happen to you? I mean these horrible changes?"

"Oh, my feet were soooo big." Sammie held out her hands a foot apart and laughed. "Almost overnight. Ma just kept putting socks on my feet because she didn't want to buy new shoes. Especially if I wasn't walking in them."

"But, I *am* walking." She looked at her sister to see if she had hurt her feelings again. "What I mean is I must have shoes. Oh, Sammie," she suddenly slumped to the floor in a little heap, the tight nightdress still half on.

"I wish Ma and Pa were here. Ma would order new shoes for me, or Pa would go into town and buy me a new pair. I miss them so much. Are they coming back? I'm scared that something bad is going to happen."

"Don't be scared. Of course, they're coming back. You heard what the trapper said. They just got delayed. It's going to be okay. We just have to have…faith. Here, let me see that nightdress. We might be able to let out the seam a bit. Or, you know what? We still have the clothes and shoes I grew out of. Maybe some of them will fit you now.

Do you remember the lavender dress with the little flowers? When you were just a tiny girl, you'd tell me I was 'so pretty' when I wore it. Let's see if it fits you now."

Sammie went into the chest at the foot of her mother's bed and dug out a few things. Holding up one of the nightdresses, she sniffed it and closed her eyes. The pleasant violet scent her mother kept in the trunk filled her nostrils and brought back memories of better times.

Sammie wondered if there would be better times in the future. She was beginning to doubt it. With her mother's broken back, she started to believe that things would never be the same again.

# Chapter Seventeen

## Guardian Angels

The next afternoon the girls cut hay in the field. They didn't notice the Indian watching them from the trees.

Sammie wiped her forehead and leaned back in her chair and, for the first time, caught sight of the tall, ominous Indian. He had a handsome, lean face, with unusually light hazel eyes, and straight lustrous black hair reaching his shoulders. Standing six feet tall, his build was slender and firm, the muscles in both his arms and chest were impressive. He wasn't nearly as large, or as old as Ellie had reported. She thought that he was perhaps her age, maybe a little older; nineteen or twenty. But what did she know about Indians? Not wanting to show fear, Sammie pretended not to see him as she slowly rolled toward Ellie.

"Ellie, don't look now, but the Indian is back," Sammie whispered.

Her sister turned her head immediately to look at the mountainside.

"Don't look. Walk back to the cabin slowly. Act like we're going in for something to eat."

Sammie couldn't help herself either. Pretending to adjust the wheel on her chair, she stole a quick look in the direction of the Indian. The handsome young man stood up, waved, and smiled at her.

She ignored him like she hadn't seen the gesture. But, Ellie waved back. The Indian's smile grew. "Sammie, he's smiling and waving."

"Don't be silly; he couldn't be. And I told you *not* to look!" Sammie was exasperated by her sister's refusal to do what she was told.

"But he's friendly." Her face lit up suddenly. "He *did* stack our wood," she reasoned.

Sammie could stand it no longer and turned to look directly at the Indian. Again he smiled and waved.

Surprised and confused, Sammie turned toward her sister, "Is that the Indian you said was like eight feet tall, big…and ugly?"

"Ummmm. He looked bigger. Maybe my imagination got the better of me."

"Ugly or handsome, he's still an Indian and a stranger. Get inside. Now!"

"We don't have to be afraid of him. He looks only a year or two older than you."

"He's an Indian. Remember what Pa taught us about them. Now move."

The two girls moved to the cabin.

Little did Sammie know that 'the big ugly Indian' had been keeping watch over them since their parents' departure. He was also curious about how the girls were managing to make it on their own. He had grown to admire how Sammie dealt with everything despite her handicap.

Every morning for the next seven days, Sammie discovered fresh flowers in a beautiful pottery cup, and freshly cut wood neatly piled on the porch.

The first morning she piled the firewood on her lap and brought it inside, then came back and took the flowers out of the pottery and into the cabin. Searching through the cupboard, Sammie found one of her mother's china vases and carefully arranged the colorful flowers in the jar, then set it on the table. She thought they gave the room more life and enjoyed looking at them during her kitchen chores. She could not figure out why the Indian would do such a thing. Her pa never told her this would happen. She wondered if it was a tribal custom and what it meant. The next morning, and every morning from then on, she would bring in the wood and the new fresh flowers, more thankful to, and increasingly curious about the Indian.

A week later, as Sammie cut hay in the field, she spotted the Indian sitting further down the hill, closer to the farm. He waved at her once again.

Sammie didn't know what to do. She knew the Indian had to be the one bringing wood and flowers every morning. Has he tricked her by pretending to be their friend, or was he a friendly Indian who simply was interested in meeting new people.

She looked up at him, still sitting on the mountainside like a guardian angel.

*****

When they arrived in Aspen, Ben stopped the wagon in front of the Sheriff's office and walked inside. At the sound of the door opening, the Sheriff looked up from a batch of new wanted posters that had arrived on the morning stage.

"Howdy, stranger, what can I do for you?"

Ben took off his hat and held it in his hands. "The name's Benjamin McPherson. I was told you have a doctor visiting – a back specialist?"

"That we do." The sheriff stood up. "Go right down this street, then turn. Aw heck, it's been a slow morning. I'll take you down there myself."

"Thank you kindly," Ben said, putting his hat back on. "My wife and I are farmers. She fell from the hayloft; I think she broke her back. We traveled to Independence, but the doc there had just passed. Then we heard about the specialist, so we headed here as fast as we could."

While they talked, the two men walked outside to the wagon.

"Your place is outside Independence?"

"Yes, sir, about forty miles."

"That's quite a haul, especially with an injured wife." The sheriff looked into the wagon and doffed his hat. "Afternoon, ma'am, your husband tells me you took quite a nasty fall."

Ellen smiled. "I did. I wasn't paying close enough attention, and, well, I paid the price."

"Lucky for you, we have a specialist visiting." He turned to Ben. "If you don't mind, I'll just hop aboard and show you where old Doc's place is. The specialist is staying there."

"That's mighty kind of you, sheriff," Ben said.

They traveled through the central part of town, and then made a turn and continued until they reached a few private homes.

"Here we are," the sheriff said, pointing to a white clapboard two-storied house on the left side of the road. The sign in the front window declared the home to belong to the resident doctor, Dr. Elroy Harrison.

The sheriff jumped down and walked into the house, while Ben opened the back of the wagon and pulled his wife's make-shift stretcher towards the end.

"Morning, Sheriff," Mrs. Harrison greeted him. "Feeling a bit under the weather?"

"Mornin', Gertrude, nope, I'm right as rain, but I got a visitor from the other side of Independence to see that specialist fellow staying with you. His wife fell from the hayloft, and her husband believes she may have broken her back."

"Oh my, tsk, tsk, Elroy, you and Doc Mayfield need to come outside. Got a woman with a possible broken back," she called out to her husband as she followed the sheriff outside.

Her husband and the other doctor quickly joined them. After making introductions, Doc Mayfield climbed inside the back of the wagon. He glanced at Ben before turning to Ellen.

"Glad to see you knew to secure your wife to a solid stretcher. Had you not done so, her injuries could have been far worse."

"It was my daughter who suggested that. We are originally from back East where she wanted to become a doctor. I bought her a mess of medical books so she could continue her studies out here. She's a smart girl," Ben said proudly.

The doctor looked down at Ellen. "So, my dear, took a nasty fall, did we?"

"Well, I don't know about you, but I sure did," she said with a grin.

"Haha, you got me there." He turned toward the others. "While we have the four of us here, let's get her out of this wagon and carry her inside to one of the spare bedrooms," Doc Mayfield told them.

"I'll go and turn the bed back," Gertrude said.

Moving very carefully, the four men carried Ellen on her board, stretcher inside to a bedroom on the first floor, and laid it on top of the bottom sheet. Everyone left the room but Ben and the doctor.

Ben watched, as Doc Mayfield gently, but thoroughly examined his wife. He tried to warn her if he thought what he was going to do would hurt. There were times when she cried out. He would stop, apologize, and tell her to take quick short breaths. When he finished the examination, he smiled and patted her arm, then asked Ben to stand next to the bed so he could address them both.

"It's good you came here. God was with you," the Doc said.

"Can you help her?" Ben asked anxiously.

"Yes, I believe I can." He looked down at Ellen. "You will have to wear a rather awkward body cast from under your arms to about here," he touched the top of her legs, "For six to eight weeks. Once we cover this area with plaster, it will take 72 hours to dry, but after that, you won't have to stay on your back all the time. With help, you can get up and walk around, even sit for short periods. Rest and sleep are critical, that's how your body heals, so I want you to get a lot of rest. And stay out of the hayloft!"

Ellen laughed. She was thrilled with his diagnosis, prescribed treatment, and his sense of humor.

"Oh, thank you! I wish I could hug you! I was afraid I'd be confined to bed for the rest of my life. I'm so tired of staring at the ceiling," Ellen exclaimed.

"When the cast comes off, will the bones be healed?" Ben asked.

"Yes," Doc Mayfield replied. "From what I could feel, she doesn't appear to have a major break, but I believe she has at least one fracture at about the middle of her back. As long as her spinal cord wasn't injured, and I don't think it was since she isn't experiencing any paralysis, she should be almost as good as new. However," he turned again to Ellen, "You may experience some lingering pain. There are a lot of nerves around the spine, and unfortunately, we won't know if any were damaged until after the cast comes off. If all is well, and I suspect it will be, I shall come to collect that hug!"

"Bless you, Dr. Mayfield," Ellen said. "You have saved my life."

"Don't give me credit," he said. "I don't heal. God heals. He just uses my hands sometimes."

# Chapter Eighteen

## Encounters

It took quite some time to form the cast around Ellen's torso. And for twelve hours, she couldn't move an inch while in the initial drying stage. Gertrude took good care of her every day. Some of the ladies from the local church stopped by every day to pray for and with her.

Now that Ben knew Ellen was going to be alright, his mind turned toward Sammie and Ellie. He wasn't happy about leaving the girls alone for so long, but they'd had no choice. Ellen would have to stay here for six weeks until she was better and had the cast taken off. He wouldn't take any chances of bringing her back in the wagon if she wasn't completely healed. Doc Mayfield showed Dr. Harrison what he would need to do to remove the cast when the time was right. He also spoke at length about physical therapy and massage, and he showed both Elroy and Ben how to do it.

The doc left for Independence ten days after Ellen's cast was set. Ben asked the doctor to tell the sheriff about Ellen, and maybe if someone was out toward the farm, they could stop, check on the girls and let them know where they were.

**** 

The next day, when Sammie left the cabin, she smiled with new appreciation at the firewood and flowers in the pottery. She went about her morning chores, but she couldn't help thinking about the handsome Indian. Slowly her heart was softening toward him – without a word between them. When she left the barn and wheeled over to the cabin, she looked at the spot the Indian sat the day before. He was there.

97

Sammie immediately turned her head back toward the cabin. She knew he had seen her and felt her cheeks get hot. She pushed her wheelchair further but couldn't help looking in his direction again. He smiled and leaned forward, turning his palms up in his lap, cocking his head to one side.

Sammie didn't know what to do until she looked over at the flowers and cut wood. *If he was going to hurt us*, she thought, *he would have done it by now.* She looked up with a small smile and waved him down to the yard.

Fast and agile, the Indian ran toward her, jumping over broken tree branches, his pace eating up the distance in no time at all. Then he realized she had moved her chair back, and he was scaring her. So he slowed to a walk and stopped eight feet away, allowing Sammie to study him.

His healthy, muscular body struck the young farm girl. It troubled her until she looked into his hazel eyes. He looked back with confidence and kindness. She even detected tenderness in his eyes. He wore a breechcloth and deerskin leggings, and although it was a bit chilly, his chest was bare. A three-inch scar on his left bicep caught her attention, making him look down to see where her attention had gone.

Sammie blushed and looked away, then turned back to meet his astonishing hazel eyes. *Hazel? But I thought Indians all had brown eyes.*

He said nothing about the surprise he saw on her face. He simply smiled, revealing his perfect white teeth.

Sammie smiled back. Her mind tried to remember some of the Indian words she was aware of from that region. While she was thinking, he simply smiled and attempted to string the phrases she knew into proper sentences.

After her first attempt, Sammie studied him to see if he understood. He turned his face slightly to one side; the confusion was written all across his face.

Sammie tried again, hoping this time, her message would be conveyed properly.

However, she only saw even more confusion in his hazel eyes. Frustrated, she searched her memory for the right words.

She tried to ask a simple question, *Who are you?* After her third attempt, there was a long pause until the Indian replied:

"You just asked me if I wore my mother's clothing," he said in perfect English.

Sammie's eyes blinked rapidly in surprise. "I didn't mean to ask you that."

"Well, the answer is 'no' if you did mean to ask." He smiled disarmingly.

'You speak English!" Sammie said with more surprise than she intended.

"Yes," he chuckled in reply.

Her eyes widened, and then she laughed. "What's your name?

"Takoda."

"How do you know English?"

"My mother taught me."

*Did your hazel eyes also come from your mother?* she wondered, but she wasn't brave enough to ask him. "Thank you for bringing the wood – and the flowers."

"I saw that it was hard for you, in the chair," Takoda replied.

She was embarrassed and looked down.

"I'm sorry, did I insult you?"

"No, of course not." She said, "My name is Samantha, but everyone calls me Sammie. You've been watching us for a while. Why?"

"Your parents left. I've been…" He searched for the right word, "…concerned for you and your sister."

"Were those moccasins by the lake yours?"

"You mean the ones you stole from me at the lake, and then left on your porch."

"We didn't mean to, but we were so surprised to find them and…."

"I was just teasing you." He smiled again, hoping to show his humor.

Sammie smiled, "Oh."

"I ran off when you and your sister came to the lake. I didn't want to frighten you.

"That night, it was you that came to the cabin to get them."

"I wouldn't have come that close, but my moccasins were on your porch, and they are the only pair I own that fit. I didn't mean to scare you."

"Maybe you should have left a note?" She blushed. She was not aware if he could write or if he even had any paper or writing implements. She wondered if she had insulted him.

"I'll certainly take that into consideration the next time some little girls steal my moccasins," he teased her once again.

"I'm not a little girl. I'm eighteen."

"Oh, I didn't mean you, of course, your little sister. Ellie is her name, right? I often hear you calling to each other. You take excellent care of her."

Sammie thought that was a kind thing for him to say, even though she didn't feel it was very accurate. She started to relax and enjoy their conversation.

"Do you have any brothers or sisters?"

"Yes, a younger sister. She's seventeen. I don't know if she could run this ranch like you have over the past few weeks." He paused and looked around.

"Sammie, would you let me help you, at least until your parents come back?" He immediately saw the pride in Sammie's face and quickly added. "Just for the more burdensome chores, or when you need something done that you can't do. "

Sammie felt a sudden sense of relief and apprehension at the same time. *Help, real help. That would be so wonderful.* But, how could she accept something like that – from an Indian, especially after her pa had warned her? But, he never met *this* Indian. He was different. She was turning all these things over in her mind, trying to be responsible, but also understanding how helpful he could be. The reality of their situation was a bit overwhelming. Maybe he was sent here to help her. *I have to make a decision*, she thought.

"Well, I guess we could use some help. As long as you're sitting up there on the hillside, you might as well."

"That's good. I would like to do that." He took her hand and pressed it between his and Sammie did her best to hide a shiver. "I'll come back tomorrow."

The Indian turned, and with another friendly wave and smile started up the hill, then broke into a run. He turned again to wave and then disappeared beyond the tree line. Two minutes later, Sammie heard a cry out in the distance. It was a cry of happiness, and she found herself smiling, and looking forward to tomorrow.

# Chapter Nineteen

## Good Times and Bad Times

Four weeks turned into six in Aspen, Colorado.

To pay for their room and board, Ben worked around the property, fixing things Gertrude told him to. It was an excellent trade.

"He's a wonderful doctor, my Elroy, but when it comes to fixing things around the house, he's all thumbs," she said. "Why these steps have needed mending for three years! Everyone knows to just walk around the edges! Mercy! People will have to retrain themselves to come up with the stairs proper!"

When Ben finished Ms. Gertrude's chores, folks around town were so impressed with his work; they hired him for their projects. When he wasn't working, Ben was with his wife, helping her to walk around the house or sit in a chair, which was more precarious. Every night he lovingly massaged her legs and arms, and Ellen would sigh with contentment and gratitude.

The church women were there every day. They brought their sewing and crochet work, discussed a variety of topics; the latest fashion, their children, recipes, the ever-changing town politics. They laughed about their lives. But, they also dug down deep to talk about their individual journeys, their search for fulfillment, and their faith in God. They shared their own trials and encouraged Ellen with stories of loss, pain, and God's enduring, unfailing love. She grew to love them as sisters, especially Gertrude, who seemed to anticipate her needs and took care of her with such joy.

People in that town were so generous with their time and attention that Ben started to rethink his attitude about God. As his wife got better and had less and less pain, he began attending Sunday services with her. The first Sunday they came, Ellen, walking oh so slowly in her cast, her hand tucked securely in his arm, the whole congregation stood and applauded. And whenever Ben was at the Harrisons, he would bow his head and join them in prayer. Ellen would silently thank God for what he was doing in Ben's life and looked for every opportunity to encourage and support him as he opened his mind and heart to God.

One Sunday afternoon, the preacher and his wife came to dinner. Afterward, he and Ben took a walk to talk about Ben's growing faith.

"I never believed in the existence of God," Ben began. "Ellen always has, though. No matter what's come our way, I've never seen her waver in her faith and trust in God. She'd read the Bible to our children every night, and in the morning as well. I used to scoff at her whenever she said that God would make everything right. Our family has been through so much. First, our eldest daughter, crippled since birth, unable to walk. She's a wonderful girl, with her mother's beautiful spirit. Never let that fact slow her down, but it breaks my heart to see her in a wheelchair or pulling herself through the dirt when she works in the garden, unbelievably one of her favorite pastimes. She loves the garden. Ellen has prayed for her to be healed, to be able to walk. But when nothing happened to make Sammie any better, I figured if there was a God, he just didn't give a hoot about our daughter or us.

"And then, we lost our son. We lived in New York City. We had the finest doctors, the best care. But he struggled with the cough and couldn't breathe. Whooping cough. How can you believe in a God who lets a child suffer so and then lets him die?"

"So, you've had a lot of bitterness and doubt to overcome."

"Yes."

"God is always with us. He hears our every word, knows our every desire, sees our pain, and yes, He does answer our prayers. Many times His answer isn't exactly what we're looking for. We think we know what we need, but we don't always. He has reasons for the things He does, and He always knows what is best for us. But we can be so set on what we think we should have, that we don't always recognize the answer He's given us."

"When Joshua died, do you know what Ellen said? She said, 'Ben, he was never ours. God just gave him to us to love for a little bit. He was a gift for all those years. He's with Jesus for now, but we'll see him again.'" Ben's voice broke as he looked up at his friend, the pastor. "Oh. . . that what she says is true. I want to believe."

"If he knew Jesus, and Ellen tells me he did, then it is true. Ben, I've watched you struggle and grow since you've been here with us, and I've prayed that the Lord would help you find the way. But I can see that He started that process long ago through Ellen. She has been pointing you lovingly toward the Savior, for a very long time. Are you ready to accept who He is? Has He convinced you yet?"

Ben stopped to look at the pastor.

"He has," Ben responded. "I'm just thankful He didn't give up on me."

"He never will, Ben. Jesus suffered terrible pain to save us all. He won't give up on us, even when we don't believe it."

The two men spoke for over an hour, and when they returned to the doctor's house, they shook hands.

"See you Sunday?"

Ben nodded. "I'll be there."

****

Sammie and Ellie now had to spend more time in the kitchen, preparing the food they had harvested for storage and use over the winter. Most of the remaining outside work, other than routine chores, consisted of picking the fruit trees clean. That morning, Ellie concentrated on the remaining apple, peach, and pear trees. Some of the fruit was turned into preserves. While the rest was sliced and canned for baking and just everyday eating.

Usually, the excess fruit and vegetables the family didn't need was sold in town and used to purchase other staples like coffee, flour, sugar, and other items. They were running low on all of those things, but since they couldn't get to town and had to make everything stretch as best they could.

While the girls were working in the kitchen, they heard a knock on the door.

"I brought you something," Takoda said as he stood in the doorway, holding a large fish.

"Fresh fish! What a treat! Thank you, Takoda," Sammie stammered, surprised at his generous gift.

As Takoda entered the cabin, he handed the fish to Ellie.

"Keep them in water until they're clean, so they don't die. Do you know how to clean them?" He asked Sammie.

"Of course. What a beautiful, fat fish," Sammie grinned up at him.

"You're welcome. There's plenty of fish, I *like* to fish, and I want to help you,"

105

his expression so earnest, his eyes sincere.

Sammie blushed. "Why would you do that?"

"Because in addition to fish, I like you…and your little sister," he said. "You are both brave and strong."

"Will you stay and eat with us?" Ellie asked, coming back from putting the fish in a bucket.

"I would like that," Takoda replied. "I came right from the lake, let me tie up my horse."

They watched as he went out to the yard to his horse. But instead of tying him to the front post, he suddenly vaulted onto his back and rode away.

"Hey, Takoda!" Ellie yelled.

"Why did he leave?" Sammie asked.

Confused, the two looked at each other as he rode into the forest. And then across the farm, they saw someone approaching.

"Is that the trapper?" Ellie asked quietly.

Through the field, the trapper was walking toward the cabin.

Sammie looked at her sister, "Go to your room and make sure your rifle is loaded."

Reaching down, Sammie turned in her chair, chambered a bullet, and laid the rifle on her lap. Then she forced herself to be calm, rolled out on the front porch, and waited on the trapper until he reached the porch.

"Mornin' Miss Samantha," Dugger called out as he tipped his hat to her, a gesture he played trying to lure her into a false sense of security.

"Morning, Mr. Dugger."

"Parent's back yet?"

Sammie didn't know how to answer the question. She had a bad feeling about him but thought perhaps that was foolish because he had saved her life.

"Expecting them any day."

"Hate to bother you, but I had a little accident, and I'm hurt. My trap closed down on my arm. If I could just bother you for some fresh water to wash up and clean my wound, that would really help me out."

He showed her his arm.

"It's infected," Sammie said, concerned. "I'll treat it with disinfectant and bandage it for you, but then you'll have to move on. Just wait here, I'll be right back."

Going into the house, she saw Ellie watching her from her bedroom doorway. "Stay in your room, close the door, and keep quiet."

"You aren't going to let that man in here, are you?" her sister whispered.

"No, I'll take care of it on the porch. Just stay out of sight."

Gathering the supplies she needed, Sammie poured some water into a basin and set it in her lap with some clean linen rags, soap, and ointment, then joined the injured trapper on the porch.

"Take a seat and let me see what I can do."

"That's right kind of you."

He sat down in the wooden rocker and held out his arm so Sammie could clean and bandage the wound. She was glad the trapper didn't know about Ellie's presence.

Dugger, however, was well aware of Sammie's little sister. Their mother had told him about two daughters, and he had seen Ellie peeking out the window from behind the curtains.

"Don't know if you've heard. But, a band of renegade Indians has been attacking some of the white settlers on their farms. You know how to use that thing?" he asked, nodding toward the rifle in her lap.

"My Pa taught me. I can shoot a cricket off the side of that tree from here." She pointed to a tree a good 50 feet away.

"That's mighty impressive," Dugger replied. He wasn't sure if he believed her. However, when he looked into her eyes, he knew she could do exactly what she said she could.

"You know, I have a girl about your age. She lives in Springfield, Ohio. Once I'm done huntin', I'll be headin' back to her and her ma for the winter," Dugger lied. "I miss them both somethin' fierce. Soon as I get me a few more hides to sell, I'll have enough to take care of my family for the rest of the fall and winter."

While he talked about his non-existent family, Sammie cleaned, disinfected, and then carefully examined his injured forearm, causing him to wince with pain.

"The bone appears to be fractured. I'll need to splint it, and you'll have to wear a sling," Sammie told him. "Would you fetch me two pieces of wood about so long and so wide from the barn," she held her hands apart, showing him the size she needed.

"Sure thing."

While he was gone, she went inside and found a piece of fabric, then tore off a large enough piece to make the sling. She was waiting for him when he returned. Wrapping the arm tightly to hold the bone together, she splinted it and helped him with the sling.

"Mind if I sleep in your barn tonight? I'm mighty tired."

Sammie hesitated, but after listening to him talk about his family, she began to trust him, just a bit. "Well..."

"I promise. I'll be gone by sunrise. I just need to recover a bit from my injury, and then I'll be out of your hair."

"I guess it will be alright, just for tonight. You can eat supper with us as well."

"The good Lord will bless you for it. He always does," Dugger said.

"Give and get, that's what my Momma taught me."

He smiled. As the trapper headed back to the barn to store his gear, she looked out over the horizon but saw no sign of the Indian.

For dinner that evening, Sammie did not serve the fish. She wanted to share that particular treat with Takoda. However, the trapper had snared a couple of rabbits that day, so Sammie made a delicious rabbit stew. Everything seemed fine at first, although Ellie was not happy about having the trapper scaring Takoda off, so she was unusually quiet.

Halfway through the meal, Dugger picked up his knife and looked around the large main room. "Kinda dangerous, you and your sister livin' out here all alone."

Sammie instantly went on alert. Her eyes darted toward her rifle, which she'd left propped against the wall near the kitchen sink. She tried not to make it visible, but the trapper saw the movement, and a slow grin spread across his face.

"You're both such pretty girls. Wouldn't want my little girl alone out here."

"We're not alone. I am seeing a gentleman. He calls quite often, been keeping an eye on us," she lied, hoping to protect herself and her sister. "He's from the farm just over the way."

"Sure, I know that farm. Passed it a ways back." He smiled. "Not far."

Both knew they were lying.

Now Sammie wanted him out of the house, and she tried to end the meal as quickly as possible. Collecting the dirty dishes, she rolled to the sink and placed them inside, prepared to grab her rifle. While her back was turned to him, he stood up and walked over to her, still holding the eating knife in his right hand.

Sammie was trapped. He stood so close she was unable to move her chair.

Dugger raised the hand with the knife. Frantic, Ellie ran for the rifle in her room. Unable to draw a single breath, Sammie watched as the knife was raised above her head and then with a quick jerk, stabbed downward. She waited for the pain. But the blade sunk into the counter, pinning a giant spider to the wood only inches from her hands. She nearly fainted when she realized it was a brown recluse, the deadliest spider known, and that he had probably saved her life yet again. The breath she withheld whooshed out of her lungs.

"Sorry for the fright. That bugger nearly got you."

"Thank…you," Sammie stammered, signaling her sister to go back to her room. "I'll get you some blankets and a lantern."

\*\*\*\*

Hidden on the mountainside, Takoda looked down on the cabin. He quickly turned his head when he heard someone running down the hill. A young Indian boy approached him.

110

"Your father requests your presence at the tribal council," the boy said.

Knowing he couldn't refuse, Takoda looked back down at the cabin. Everything seemed peaceful and quiet. If anything was wrong, he knew Sammie would have yelled. He hesitantly left his spot and headed back up the hill. No one disobeyed the chief, especially if he was your father.

**** 

As the sisters slept that night, Dugger returned to the house and snuck through the window of their parents' room. Using the lantern, he quietly searched the bedroom and the main room. Dugger pocketed the girls' mother's jewelry, including a necklace she kept in a small box on top of her dresser. He smiled as he examined it in the light of the lantern. That would bring him more than a pocket of coins. He bit down on it. Oh yes, solid gold, just like his front tooth.

He moved into the kitchen area and took their best cutting knife and a container of oil for the lantern. He picked up the large leather Bible. The book would also bring in a reasonable amount of money. Although, he put it back, afraid that stealing a Bible would bring him bad luck. Leaving through the front door, he packed the stolen goods and the blankets on Gypsy, the girls' only remaining horse, threw himself into the stolen saddle, and rode off.

He was gone long before sunrise.

# Chapter Twenty

## Unexpected Kindness

The next morning Sammie found herself on the front porch early, hoping the trapper would be gone as promised. When she saw the barn door open, she had an odd feeling that something was wrong. Sammie pushed herself down the ramp and toward the barn, her emotions ranging from fear to anger.

"The chickens better not be gone because Dugger was too lazy to close the barn door," she said aloud.

When she finally got inside, she headed straight for the chickens and let out a sigh of relief. They were all there. She quickly gathered the eggs.

"Mr. Dugger, are you still here?"

Daisy mooed, but that was the only sound she heard.

"Mr. Dugger? Would you like some breakfast before you go?"

Nothing.

*He must have left, just as he promised,* she thought. To be sure, she rolled over to the stalls to check the cows and Gypsy. Annabelle and Daisy munched contentedly on their hay while the calf suckled his mother's milk. "And how are you feeling today, Gypsy?" She turned in her chair. "Gypsy?"

Their beautiful, painted horse was gone.

"Gypsy!"

Sammie checked his stall, in case the horse was lying down, but it was empty. Then she checked the pasture. No horse.

Anger welled up inside until she was ready to burst. "Doggone it, that no good, black-hearted, two timing-son-of-a-motherless-goat! !" She went back inside the barn to see what else was missing. Gypsy's saddle and bridle were also gone. She couldn't climb the ladder to the loft, but Sammie was willing to bet, he had taken their blankets and the lantern as well.

Returning to the cabin, she wheeled inside when the door to her parent's room moved slightly. Too angry to be afraid, Sammie chambered a bullet in her rifle and shoved the door back open with the foot of her chair. She aimed and quickly examined the room. No one was inside, but the window was wide open, and the breeze blowing through it was brisk enough to flutter the curtains and move the door.

She closed the window and secured it; then she took inventory of the room and its contents. Drawers were partially open, and their contents rifled through. Her mother's jewelry box was open, and everything was gone, including her mother's most precious necklace. Checking the closet, she discovered her father's new boots were missing along with his winter coat. By the time she headed into the kitchen, Sammie was furious, especially angry at herself for trusting the old buzzard. How would she explain this to Ma and Pa? They would be so disappointed.

She checked the cookie jar. The money inside was missing. *Gone!* "At least he didn't take the good silver, too," she grumbled as she slammed the pantry drawer.

Ellie wandered into the kitchen, coughing and rubbing her eyes. "What's going on?" She asked, trying to stifle another harsh cough. "Why are you making so much noise?"

"The trapper robbed us blind, Ma's jewelry, some of Pa's clothes, and his good boots, along with all the money we had left in the house."

"I told you! I told you not to trust him," Ellie fumed.

"I know." Sammie's face seemed to crumble.

"Now, what are we going to do?" Ellie demanded. "You should have listened to Pa!"

"Yes, Ellie, I know!" Sammie's words were firm and angry, but then her shoulders sagged in defeat. "I made a horrible decision."

"Ma and Pa are really going to be upset when they come home and find everything missing."

"They never should have trusted me with the farm. I'm nothing but a failure."

Sammie left the house and pushed herself angrily across the property, passing the fields, and heading toward the lake. It wasn't easy, and every time the chair got hung up, she ranted and raved at it. Hot tears running down her face, she wiped at them with the back of her hand.

Back at the cabin, putting her hand over her mouth, Ellie felt another cough coming on and went to the water bucket. She was so thirsty, and her throat was sore. Ellie poured a cup, but when she brought it to her mouth, another horrible cough overwhelmed her, and she dropped the cup. Unable to stop the hacking spasm, she doubled over, fighting to catch her breath.

At the lake, Sammie took her anger and frustration out by pounding the arm of her wheelchair. "Stupid chair, I hate you! You make everything hard. It would have been better if I had never been born." She bowed her head and cried in choking sobs.

"It would not have been better," a soft male voice told her.

She knew that voice and looked up.

Takoda walked out from the tree and knelt in front of her.

"Did you hear what I said?"

"Yes," but her expression said otherwise.

He lifted her from the chair and carefully set her down on the ground, her back against a tree. As embarrassed as she was, his strong arms and gentle voice gave her comfort.

Sammie looked at his face. "He…he…stole the horse. He…stole…everything," she hiccupped.

"I know. I heard you tell your sister it was your fault." He paused. "Sammie, you were kind and compassionate. You are a good person."

"Am I?"

"Yes. You didn't know that the trapper would take advantage. You trusted him because you are trustworthy."

"I should have known. I should have been more responsible."

"I am sorry he stole from you. He tricked you."

Takoda reached out and touched her arm, startling Sammie with a most pleasant feeling. She hoped he didn't notice the involuntary shiver. After all, he was only an Indian.

"Here," he said, "wipe your eyes."

She took the small piece of soft cloth from him. As she looked up to thank him, she was struck by the compassion in his eyes. He looked at her with such warmth and friendliness that Sammie's heartbeat an extra beat. *What was this?* She was afraid to even think about it.

"I am sorry I left."

"Where did you go?"

"I didn't want the trapper to see me. He could have created a lot of trouble – for both of us. I was on the hillside until I was summoned to the village. There has been trouble with some renegade tribes attacking white settlers. The meeting went on for most of the night. I would never have left you alone if I had thought anything like this would happen."

She handed the small piece of cloth back to Takoda. "Thank you. I didn't know Indian's carried handkerchiefs." She looked at him, puzzled.

The Indian laughed. "My mother insists. I believe I am the only Indian who carries one. She says, 'All real gentlemen carry a handkerchief.' She attempts to make me more civilized." Takoda picked up Sammie in his arms and placed her gently in the chair. "It's time to get you back to the cabin."

Once more, Sammie's felt her heartbeat loudly. *He must hear it,* she thought as she tried to slow her racing heart, but she couldn't. It beat even faster with every turn of the wheel, as he pushed her toward the cabin. He steered her toward the kitchen and what would prove to be the first fun and relaxing evening she had experienced in a long time.

Ellie stood back from Sammie, feeling somewhat ashamed for being angry at her. Takoda helped break the tension when he asked if he could help them with their chores, and then immediately chose Ellie to assist him.

It was one of the most pleasant afternoons the girls had experienced. Takoda's presence made everything more fun. Ellie didn't complain once, and together, she and the

Indian were able to get all of the outside chores done, plus cut, split and stack a good amount of firewood.

By late afternoon, everyone was tired, and as Takoda and Ellie washed up at the kitchen sink, Takoda explained to both the girls that when an Indian worked hard, he expected to be fed well and have the rest of the day off to play.

"That," Ellie said, "is an exquisite custom to have."

"I've already started supper." Sammie threw Takoda a clean towel to dry his hands. " The vegetables are cooking and…" She paused for effect. "We have some fresh, tasty fish seasoned and ready for the skillet."

"What? You didn't feed the trapper, our fish?" Takoda exclaimed. "Why, Sammie McPherson, how un-hospitable of you!'"

He laughed a wonderful deep laugh, and the girls realized they were about to have an exceptional evening, just the three of them. Takoda left late, and the girls went right to bed, feeling safe and at peace.

# Chapter Twenty-One

## Fishing Lessons

The next morning when Sammie left the house, she discovered in addition to the usual stack of daily firewood, an unusually large, beautiful bouquet of wildflowers in vivid blues, deep purples, and bright oranges and yellows. It had been a while since he'd brought her flowers, and she lifted them and breathed in their heady fragrance. Then looking across the way, she spotted Takoda in his usual place on the hillside. She waved for him to come down.

"Good morning, Sammie. I hope you're feeling better and ready for a beautiful day," Takoda said as he stepped onto the porch.

"I'm still upset about the trapper, but yes. Thanks to you, I feel much better." She smiled. "Are these flowers for me?"

Takoda grinned. "I thought they might make you smile."

"Oh, they do. They're so beautiful. Thank you."

He wanted to tell her they weren't half as beautiful as she was, but kept those thoughts to himself and enjoyed just looking at her, knowing they would spend the day together.

"Would you and Ellie like to learn how to fish today?"

Having overheard them talking, Ellie ran through the front door. "Yes, yes, yes! " A raspy cough cut into her enthusiasm. "Cough, cough, I would, I would, I would! Teach me to fish, Takoda!"

When she saw Takoda and Sammie looking at her and grinning, she blushed.

"What I mean is, both of us, right Sammie? We both want to learn?"

Her coughing was worse, deeper sounding, and Sammie was a little worried. This morning at breakfast, she'd coughed so long her face turned red.

"I don't know. Maybe you should just spend the day in bed. Your cold seems to be getting worse."

"No, please, Sammie. As long as I rest, what difference does it make? Fishing is restful. Isn't it Takoda?" She didn't want Sammie to know she had a sore throat as well. Maybe fishing would take her mind off it.

"Fishing is so restful that it sometimes puts people to sleep," he agreed, siding with Ellie.

Sammie looked at her sister long and hard, wanting to make the right decision. Ellie tried her best not to cough while her big sister was watching, and finally, Sammie smiled and gave in.

"As long as you don't run around and truly rest, I suppose we can go. Why don't I make a picnic lunch, and we can enjoy a lazy afternoon together."

"What will we need to catch the fish?" Ellie asked.

"I have everything we need waiting by the lake," Takoda said, "Including the fish."

Ellie could barely contain her excitement. She helped Sammie put together their lunch and pack it in a basket. She was about to go to her room to change into her swim dress, but Takoda stopped her.

"No, Ellie, if you swim, you will scare all the fish away," he teased her with a stern look.

"But I...."

"Do you want to fish or swim?" Takoda asked.

"Fish, I guess. But does that mean I can't swim in the lake anymore?"

"Only when you have a bad cold, and when we're trying to catch our supper," Sammie said with a smile. Takoda pushed the wheelchair, and they arrived at the lake in no time at all. He had placed the fishing gear in a canoe that rested on the shore nearby. Sammie gave him a puzzled look.

"I thought we would fish from the shore."

"We wouldn't catch much of anything there. So I brought my canoe from across the lake," Takoda replied.

"I don't know. What if the boat tipped over? I can't swim."

"Don't worry so much. I will set you in the canoe and keep you safe," he assured Sammie. "I am a strong swimmer, and so is Ellie. Nothing bad will happen to you."

Although her father had taken her into the water with him sometimes, Sammie was still afraid and for a good reason. Although she trusted Takoda, and after a lot of pleading on Ellie's part, which sent her into another coughing fit, she finally agreed.

"I've never been in a boat...I mean canoe before," Ellie gushed. "This is going to be so much fun."

After Takoda got Sammie settled in the canoe, Ellie got in behind her, leaving the front open for Takoda, who pushed the boat into the water and climbed in. Using a long wooden oar, he paddled the canoe further out to the middle of the lake. Then he turned around to face the girls and instructed them on how to fish. They each received a fishing lure and a spear.

"Wait," Sammie said. "We have to spear the fish? Don't you use a pole? I'm sure that's what people use."

Takoda raised his left eyebrow. "I suppose you could call this a pole, but it is actually a spear."

"No...I mean, I know it's a spear. I'm talking about a pole, a stick. Pa would tie a string with a hook to the end of a pole, and he used a worm, sometimes a cricket, for bait."

Takoda smiled. "Here, we use a spear, except when we go salmon fishing. Then we use spear points attached to a rope and a salmon plate. If we catch enough fish, I will show you how to smoke the fish we don't eat so that it will last a long time just like smoked meat."

"Oh!" Sammie loved learning new ways to do things. "Then, should we get started?" Sammie suggested.

Lowering the lure into the water, Takoda leaned over the side of the boat and stared intently. Several minutes passed before a giant fish swam into view. Lifting his arm, he took careful aim, and at just the right moment, he speared the fish and placed it in the fishing bag.

"You see. It is easy."

"My goodness! That is one big fish," Sammie said.

"I want to try next," Ellie said excitedly.

"Takoda traded places with Ellie and handed her the spear. "Just do what I did. You must be very still, and whatever you do, don't let go of the spear." Takoda showed her how to hold the spear. The hardest part was waiting for a fish to appear. It happened much quicker this time, and before long, a large fish approached the boat. Ellie started to say something, but Sammie put her finger to her lips.

"Shhh, you don't want to scare it away," she whispered.

Ellie nodded and glanced up at their guide. Takoda nodded and mouthed the word, "Now."

Bringing down the spear too fast, Ellie missed, but out of pure luck, she managed to stab once more before the fish got away.

"I got it! I got it!" she squealed. But the fished wiggled so hard; the spear slipped through her fingers. "No! Come back!"

Before anyone could stop her, Ellie reached out so far that she fell into the water with a big splash.

"Ellie!" Sammie cried out.

Spluttering about, Ellie found her way back to the side of the canoe. Takoda, with some help from Sammie, pulled her back in. While Sammie started to fret about Ellie getting more sick, Takoda began to row back to shore. "Maybe that is enough fishing for one day," he said.

"Well," Ellie coughed, "I guess I got to take a swim after all."

# Chapter Twenty-Two

## Horses and Jealousy

Sammie was excited and happy the next morning as she fixed breakfast for Ellie and herself. She had gotten up early and headed for the barn, gathering eggs and milking Daisy, before returning to the house to make breakfast. As she worked, she couldn't help singing a song her mother used to sing whenever she was happy. In between, she thought about the previous day and what a wonderful time she'd had with Takoda, despite Ellie taking an unexpected swim. He was always on her mind. *It was so sweet of him to bring me flowers,* she thought.

Setting the oatmeal, a pitcher of fresh warm milk, and a jar of peaches on the table, she opened the bedroom door and sang out, "Ellie, time to get up."

Her sister's response was a tired moan.

"Come on, Ellie, I let you sleep a little later. Got to get up. We have a lot of chores to do today."

Silence.

Sammie rolled her chair into the bedroom. "Come on, sleepyhead. We have to repair that break in the pasture fence before we can let the cows out to graze."

"Let me sleep a little longer. I'm so tired."

Sammie pulled the covers off Ellie. "No, get up now. It's late, and there is so much to do."

Ellie groaned and dragged herself out of bed, stumbling to the washbasin to wash her face. "I hate living on a farm. It's stupid! Why do we have to get up so early? I hate cows."

"Really? You hate cows?"

Ellie coughed. "Yes, I hate cows and chickens, too. They're too much work."

"That is so immature," Sammie called over her shoulder as she rolled out of the room.

"Yeah? Well, I'm twelve…no wait. I forgot I had a birthday that we never celebrated. I'm thirteen!" She coughed again.

"Oh! I'm sorry, Ellie" She stopped and turned around to face her younger sister. "We've been so busy, and things have just been. . ." There was no excuse, and Sammie felt terrible. "I forgot. We'll celebrate Sunday." What kind of celebration would you like? *I don't even have flour to make her a cake,* she thought. *How could I have forgotten?*

After mending the fence, Sammie sent her sister to fetch water for the laundry and their needs for the day. It took forever, and she was beginning to lose lost patience with Ellie.

"If you don't hurry up with that water, the wash won't be dry until nightfall," Sammie scolded.

When Ellie finally appeared with the water, Sammie didn't notice how pale she looked. She was more concerned with doing the wash and hanging it up to dry. As she draped Ellie's favorite blue skirt over the clothesline and pushed the wooden clothespin firmly over the worn cotton, she called over her shoulder for Ellie to sweep the floors inside, as well as the porch. But her sister disappeared again, so Sammie ended up doing it herself. It wasn't easy and took twice as long. When she finished, she checked the laundry, most of it was still damp, but a few pieces were dry enough to take down. There was a slightly chilly breeze, which occasionally gusted, making the sheets snap. She held a pillowcase up to her nose after folding it. Sammie loved the fresh scent of clothes dried outside.

Placing the basket, with a few pieces of dry laundry on her lap, she returned to the house and put them away; then she rolled back out to the porch and closed her eyes, enjoying the breeze and warm sun on her face. When she opened them, Takoda was dismounting from his horse. He stepped on the ramp and approached her chair. She smiled, happy to see him. *He is very handsome.* What was she thinking? *He's a good friend and has taught us so much, that's all.* He always walked so quietly that had her eyes remained closed; she would not have been aware of his presence.

Bending down to talk to her at her level, Takoda said, "Enough chores for awhile. I believe we need an adventure today."

"Oh," she opened her eyes wide with mock alarm, "Yesterday wasn't enough of an adventure?"

He laughed, and she joined him.

"What do you have in mind, Takoda?"

"Hmm, name something you've never done."

"A lot of things," Sammie replied, feeling a little hurt.

"Oh, this thing." He touched the wheelchair. "Well, this will not be part of our adventure." He slowly looked around the farm before turning to Sammie. "Have you ever been on a horse?"

"How? No, of course not. I mean, my Pa would never let me." She paused a moment. "He didn't want me to get hurt."

Takoda's expression turned serious as he knelt in front of her and placed both hands on her knees. *His hands are so strong and yet gentle.* "Sammie, do you trust me?"

She hesitated at first, then with confidence, she replied, "Yes."

"Good. Then we are halfway there." Takoda lifted her and carried her to his horse. "Easy, Gingerbread, easy boy," His voice was gentle.

"Gingerbread? Your horse's name is Gingerbread?"

"My mother makes delicious gingerbread. It is my favorite. This has been my horse since I was six years old. I named him after my favorite treat, and of course, because of his color," he added as an acceptable reason.

Sammie laughed. "Your mother makes gingerbread? That's very…."

"Can we have this discussion after I place you on his back? You're getting a little heavy."

Sammie blushed as he lifted her shoulder height and then placed her gently on the back of the horse. Then Takoda swung up behind Sammie and put his arms around her to hold the reigns. Sammie couldn't help smiling as she felt his strong arms around her. She had never been this close to a boy before, any boy. It felt good. But she wondered if it was alright. *What if Ma or Pa were here? What would they think if they saw Takoda's arms around me…and me on a horse? Am I foolish or brave?*

"Now lean back into me. I'm going to keep you steady and balanced." When she did, he said, "Good, now try to relax. Don't be so tense. I've got you. Tch nice and slow Gingerbread."

The horse started walking, circling the yard at a leisurely pace. The experience was so new and wonderful for Sammie, she turned her head and smiled at Takoda, and mouthed the words, "Thank you." Then she turned back to enjoy the experience fully. *What freedom,* she thought. Leaning forward, she stroked Gingerbread's silky neck. *I wonder if I could learn to ride by myself?* She pictured herself on the hillside, leaning slightly forward on her horse as he broke into a slow, smooth canter through the leaves and underbrush of an early fall day. The daydream made her happy and excited at the same time. She leaned back into Takoda's arms.

As they made the second circuit, Ellie appeared from around the side of the barn. She dropped the hoe she was holding in shock.

"Sammie! Are you riding a horse? Oh my, Sammie. You're riding a horse…with an Indian!"

Sammie blushed, and Takoda pulled her closer. He raised his eyebrows, and a little smile formed on his lips as he whispered in Sammie's ear, "Sammie, you're riding a horse…with an Indian."

They both laughed.

"Yes, I am," she said proudly.

Ellie watched them for a moment, then turned back into the house. She was so thirsty and wanted to lie down for just a little while. She was angry at Sammie and a little jealous. Here she was doing all the chores while her sister rode a horse with Takoda, like some Indian princess.

Takoda took Sammie for a long ride around the lake. Sammie never felt more regular in her life. For a while, she forgot about her wheelchair. The two laughed as they rode. Takoda pointed out deer hiding in the trees, skunks running along a narrow path and blue jays high up in the pine trees. The ride ended as Takoda stopped his horse next to the porch. He jumped down and then lifted her down. He carried her back up the ramp to her chair, but he didn't set her down immediately. Instead, he pulled her closer and tighter. Their eyes locked. Sammie's expression was dreamy, as slowly she brought her face closer to his. Her heart was beating very fast, and Sammie *knew* he was going to kiss her. Then Ellie walked out on the porch.

"Why don't I fix us something to eat," Sammie said, pulling away, hoping Ellie hadn't seen anything.

Takoda gave Sammie a tender look, as he set her down in her chair.

"Sammie, I can't find the water bucket. If you want me to peel vegetables, I have to get water. But I can't get water if I can't find the water bucket. I've looked everywhere. Did you put it somewhere after you did the wash?"

Feeling a bit embarrassed by their near kiss, Sammie looked at her sister, exasperated. "I'll find it."

She headed into the cabin, but as she passed through the doorway, she looked back over her shoulder to catch his eye. He winked.

While Sammie was inside, Ellie started humming and walked up to Gingerbread.

"Sammie's *other* boyfriend has a horse, too, but he never lets her ride it like you. They mostly just sit on the porch and kiss. I don't like to watch it when they kiss." She paused as she patted the horse's neck. "He's been gone for a while, but he's coming back. I think maybe he went to the city to buy an engagement ring or something. Sammie's always talking to his photograph. He's alright, I guess, but not as nice as you." She smiled up at the frowning Indian, just as Sammie rolled out with the bucket in her lap.

"Here, Ellie." She turned to Takoda. "Would you like to come in and sit a spell?

It's cooler in here," Sammie said.

Without a word, Takoda mounted his horse, looked at Ellie, who started coughing and then at Sammie. "I have to go."

He galloped off, never looking back. Sammie waved, but he didn't see her. With a confused look on her face, she turned to Ellie,

"Hmm, I wonder what got into him," Ellie asked.

# Chapter Twenty-Three

## Family Counseling

Takoda rode as fast as Gingerbread would run. His mind was a blur of hurt, anger, and confusion. Ellie's words still rang in his ears. *"Sammie's always talking to his photograph. I don't like to watch it when they kiss."* Each word felt like the stab of a knife to his heart.

When he reached his village, he deftly slid off his horse and slapped him on the hindquarters to send him to the herd. Takoda would brush him later. Right now, he couldn't be bothered. He had never felt this way before. *I don't understand what's happening. Why would Sammie pretend to like me the way a woman does a man if she already has someone else in her life?*

He wanted to talk with his mother and ask questions. *Do white women usually act this way?* But when he entered the family's hut consisting of an oval frame covered with brushwood and grass, only his sister was there. He was about to step back outside when suddenly he found himself seeing her differently. *She is a girl around Sammie's age. Perhaps she could help me understand this.*

Her back was to him when he approached. As she weaved on a small loom, she hummed a happy tune.

"Rising Moon?"

She turned on the short little stool and smiled at her brother.

"The white farmer's daughter…" he began.

"Do you mean Samantha?"

"Yes, of course, Samantha…Sammie. She prefers Sammie. She…she has another man. He comes to visit sometimes."

Rising Moon crossed her arms and studied her older brother. "You look very upset, and that's unusual for you. Have you ever seen this man?"

"No. Never but there is a picture, I've seen that. He looks to be about my age, maybe a little younger, quite handsome and strong."

"How do you know this is someone she cares for?"

"Her sister told me, little Ellie. She said he was away for a time, perhaps buying Sammie a ring, something to signify she is his," Takoda said, miserably.

"White people call that an engagement ring. It means they will be married," Rising Moon told him.

"Dear sister, I cannot bear to think of Sammie with another man. It makes me hurt right here," he said, clutching his gut. "I don't know what to do. I've tried to impress her with my skills and strength, but she hardly seems to notice. And yet…"

"Oh, she notices, but…" Rising Moon looked at her brother and shook her head. "Sit."

Takoda quickly sat on his haunches in front of her looking into her soft brown, loving eyes. He hoped she could shed some light on this mystery, on being a girl, on Samantha.

"Here's the thing, one thing anyway. Boys see with their eyes. So you think that is how girls are made as well. And you think that strutting around like a peacock will impress her."

"Doesn't it?"

131

She shook her head. "You know what impresses a girl?

"I think you're saying I have no idea. I'm listening, go on."

"Kindness." She paused before going on. "Attention." She paused again. "Listening." She smiled and opened her eyes wide. "And sharing something beautiful."

"Like a sunset or a starry night?"

"Yes! Good, you're already learning to listen! Next, you have to learn how to communicate. Tell her what you feel in your heart. Here," she said as she gently poked the left side of his chest and gave him a little push. "Make her feel special like she is different from everyone else, and no one can take her place. She needs to know that she is the *only* one." Crouching inches from his face, she continued. "And that you..," she paused again, looking at him, then taking his chin in her hand. "Takoda, finish my sentence. She is the only one and that you..."

"That ...I love her."

"Yes!" Rising Moon jumped to her feet and clapped. Then she sat back down on the small stool and looked thoughtfully at her brother.

Takoda closed his eyes and spoke slowly.

"I do love her. I've never cared for someone or wanted to protect someone or be with someone like I do, Sammie."

"Good start. Next, do you want to spend the rest of your life with her in the same hut?"

"That would be wonderful! Yes, I do; even now, when I left her, I didn't want to. I want to always be with her."

Rising Moon gave her brother a delighted sisterly smile, "Well then, I believe you do love this girl." She turned back to work on her loom.

"But dear, dear little sister. How do I tell her? How do I let her know how I feel? And how will I know if she feels the same way I do?"

"Hmmm. . . .you do need help. Don't worry. I will help you. I will be your guide." Rising Moon slipped off her stool and sat on the large bear rug at her brother's feet, crossing her legs and bringing her hands together in a prayerful pose. "Consider me, Rising Moon, Your Indian Love Guide. And whatever you do, don't ask father about courting."

"Why not?"

"For one thing, I don't think Sammie would understand the meaning of a 'courting blanket.' It might scare her away."

"But our mother was courted in such a fashion."

"True, but she lived with the tribe first, and she had many Indian women to explain it to her. And let us be honest. What choice did she have?" She looked at him earnestly. "Think about it, Takoda. What would Sammie think if you suddenly approached her and wrapped a blanket around the two of you, especially in this heat? I think she would laugh when you explained the purpose of this was to protect you both from overprotective parents, curious onlookers, and the sun. I believe she would think you are absolutely crazy. Besides, there's no one at the farm but her little sister."

"Then what am I to do?" Takoda was clearly exasperated.

"Mother and I have spoken of this often, especially since some of the young warriors have begun to look favorably upon me. Courtship should be a spiritual matter – a faith-filled journey of joy, although sometimes painful. You must be open to God's will, and he will surely guide you to the right woman. Remember, the person you want isn't always the right one meant for you."

"So, you're saying that Sammie is meant for the other and not for me?"

"No, of course not, if I thought that I would not encourage you to court her," Rising Moon said.

Takoda sighed and stood up. "I'm still confused. I will speak to our father later. He married a white woman. He will surely know what to do."

Rising Moon laughed. "I think it wise to speak to mother as well. After all, she was the one who 'chased the chief until he caught her.'"

# Chapter Twenty-Four

## The Sickness Starts

When Ellie came to the breakfast table three days later, her coughing was significantly worse. Between coughing spells, her next breath of air sounded like a high pitched whoop. She sat down in her chair, shoved her breakfast aside, and laid her head on the table as she struggled to breathe.

A jolt of fear shot through Sammie. She had been trying to convince herself otherwise, but it was too obvious to ignore any longer. Ellie had whooping cough. Their brother had died of it years ago. And that was in New York, where they had good doctors. Sammie's sister needed medicine and a doctor, but without money or a means to get to town, there was no way to obtain either.

"Why don't you go back to bed? I'll do the chores myself this morning."

"No, I know how hard it is for you, and some things are just impossible to do alone."

Ellie sat up and picked at her egg and a slice of bread, washing it down with a cup of weak tea, then went outside to do the chores.

**** 

After the morning chores were complete, they went inside for lunch. Ellie lay down while her sister prepared it for them. She searched the cold cellar for something to tempt her sister's appetite and was thrilled when she found some salted pork and a small container of cornbread meal her mother had stored months ago on a bottom shelf. She added a freshly canned jar of green beans, an onion, and a few potatoes to the pork. When

135

lunch was ready, she woke up with her sister.

"Lunch is ready," Sammie said kindly.

"I'm not very hungry." Ellie coughed so hard; she had to clear her throat afterward.

"Try to eat as much as you can. You need to keep your strength up," Sammie said, trying to remain upbeat. "Ma and Pa depend on us. You'll feel better after you eat."

"I don't think so, Sammie." Her eyes were red and watery, and she coughed, making the whooping sound again as she struggled for her next breath. Ellie picked at her food, hardly taking a bite, just moving it slowly around her plate.

When Sammie finished eating, she busied herself cleaning up. The next time she looked at her sister, Ellie had fallen asleep at the table, still coughing in her sleep. Gently waking her, Sammie led her back to bed and felt Ellie's forehead. Her sister was running a fever.

"You're hot," Sammie gave her a loving, but worried smile. "I'll be back in a minute."

Sammie went into the small parlor to think. What should she do about Ellie's cough? She had studied enough of the medical books to know the symptoms. She had to take some action. Sammie rolled her chair into the bedroom. Seeing Ellie shiver and cough, she covered her with a quilt, inwardly berating Dugger for stealing their extra blankets. Her sister was burning up with fever, so she filled the washbasin with cold water and spent the night changing the wet cloth on Ellie's forehead whenever it got warm.

****

Near midnight, Sammie fell asleep but was awakened when Ellie began to hallucinate.

"Ma! Ma, you're back. I missed you so much," she said, looking at her sister with half-closed eyes.

"Ellie, I'm not Ma. It's me, Sammie," she said as she wrung out the cloth and wiped her sister's forehead.

"Ma, the chickens," Ellie said, laughing, but it turned into coughing. "Ma, the chickens are all dressed for Sunday church. Grandma! Hello Grandma! They're marching with Grandma to church...."

"Ellie, its Sammie. Listen, sweetie. There are no chickens. You...."

"I *love* chickens...and...cough, cows, too!"

Sammie started crying as she smoothed the sweaty hair back from Ellie's forehead.

"God, if you do exist, and if you really do care about any of us. . . if you can hear me, don't let my sister die. Send someone. Do something. Don't you let my sister die! Please!"

Exhausted, Sammie eventually fell asleep with her head on the bed next to her sister's arm until the rooster woke her up.

Ellie was quiet and still. Too still.

# Chapter Twenty-Five

## Faith and Trust

When it was time to remove the cast, Ben waited in the parlor with several church members. All prayed that Ellen would be healed. It took quite a while to remove the cast. Afterward, Dr. Elroy examined her back and left the room while his wife helped Ellen take a bath.

"Oh, this is heaven," Ellen exclaimed. "It's so wonderful to move and be rid of that itchy smelly thing."

"That itchy smelly thing gave you your life back," Gertrude told her as she gently washed her guest's back. "And it didn't smell that bad until the past couple of weeks," she teased Ellen. She pinched her fingers to her nose and shook her head. "We could smell you coming, my dear, half a block away."

"Oh, how terrible. Why didn't you say something?" Over the past weeks, the women had become fast friends, and Ellen knew she would miss Gertrude terribly when she returned to the farm. There she had no adult friends, not one. The time with Gertrude had been extraordinary. Not only had she taken care of her physically, but had listened to her, prayed with her, and made her laugh so hard at times, she thought she would bust out of her cast.

"Now, what possible good would that have done? No one wanted you to take that thing off too soon. We would have fainted from the stench before we would allow you to ditch it before it was time. Just imagine how happy everyone will be to smell the real you! And just look at you! Here, with no itchy, stinky, massive cast. Only you - healed!

Praise God!

"Yes, praise God! Gertrude…" Ellen stopped her friend's hands from washing her shoulders and took them in her own. "I am so grateful for all that you, your husband, and everyone at church have done for Ben and me. There are no words. I will be forever thankful. But especially, you, my dear friend. Thank you for your joy."

"You're very welcome," Gertrude said with a smile. "Now, let's get you dressed. A lot of people are waiting to see the new, healed, and nice smelling Ellen!"

After helping her dress in clean undergarments, Gertrude called the doctor back into the room. He was carrying what appeared to be a woman's corset in his hands. When Ellen saw it, she made a face.

"Oh, I hated wearing those things back in New York. Out here, I don't have to bother."

"Well, I'm sorry to say it, but this is your back brace. You're back is still weak, so I want you to wear this," he said.

"For how long? I'm sorry. I didn't mean to offend you. I just didn't expect it. I'll wear it. I'm so grateful that I have the chance for a normal life, even if it means wearing a corset. How long will I have to wear it?"

"Difficult to say. You may only need it for a few weeks, or it might take longer. Worst case, if you're experiencing a lot of pain and upper body weakness, you might have to wear it forever. This is more than just a corset, Ellen, Doc Mayfield fashioned it specifically for you."

The doctor and Gertrude helped her with the corset. It wasn't so bad, certainly nowhere nearly as uncomfortable as the body cast!

"There's a crowd gathering. Gertrude, you better get this lady dressed and ready."

He left the room with a smile. *It was a miracle,* he thought to himself, *a real God-almighty miracle.*

Ellen looked over at the chair in the corner where her pale yellow dress had been laid out. She hadn't been able to wear real clothing for some time. This was one of the two dresses she had brought with her. Somewhat faded, but comfortable. She'd been wearing borrowed dresses, two sizes too big over her body cast. It would be so kind to wear her old, pale yellow one.

"My dress, Gert?" She looked at the chair.

"Oh, that? You know, the girls got together..." Ellen knew she meant the women from church. "They decided you needed something new to celebrate your healed back. So." Gertrude pulled out a medium-sized box, wrapped in brown paper, and handed it to the bewildered Ellen. "For you - from your friends."

Laughing, she tore into the paper and lifted the cover of the box.

"Oh! My! It's beautiful, Gert, absolutely stunning!" She reached in and held the powder blue dress up to her and stared into the mirror. The blue material was as light as air, and the blue matched her eyes perfectly. She'd never seen such a beautiful but practical piece of clothing. "It's so light and delicate, and yet it seems so well made. The sleeves are perfect, just above my elbow. I have to try it on right now."

"Ellen! I wish everyone could see your face. Yes! You do have to try it on - and keep it on. Patience found the material while visiting in the city, and Caroline designed it, with you in mind, knowing what a farm wife has to do. Go on, go on, and put it on. Here, I'll help you."

The two women chattered and laughed as Ellen prepared herself for their friends. Inside the box, she found a small jacket made of the same material. Everything fit perfectly.

When Ellen walked into the parlor filled with people, she was glowing. The women were thrilled that their gift looked so beautiful on her. The men clapped and cheered. Ben greeted his wife, his eyes shining. She had never looked so beautiful, standing with no pain, entirely by herself, radiant in her joy and gratitude.

"Praise the Lord," he said, without even thinking.

"Amen!" Everyone replied.

****

"Ellie, Ellie!" Sammie shook her sister. She was limp and covered in sweat.

"Ellie! God, *No.* Don't you do this. Whatever you want from me. Don't, please…."

Suddenly, Ellie gasped and opened her eyes. She looked at her sister, confused, and then the coughing started again.

Ellie stayed in bed, and Sammie didn't care. *The farm and the animals be hanged,* she decided. She would do what she could and take care of Ellie. What got done got done. Sammie spoon-fed her sister more soup before heading to the barn to tackle as many chores as she could. Every evening after making sure Ellie was asleep, she sat on the porch and watched until dark for her parents to appear over the ridge. Or, for Takoda. And every night she was disappointed.

Three days later, Takoda stood on the porch. After his abrupt departure, Sammie was surprised by his visit.

"How is your sister?"

"It's hard to say. She had a really bad turn three days ago. I thought I'd lost her. But she seems to be a little better. I'm just not sure. The whooping cough is as bad as ever, and she sleeps most of the day. Her fever breaks, but then it comes back."

Sammie wanted to throw herself into Takoda's arms and have a good cry. She wanted him to comfort her and say it would be alright. She wanted him to say he'd help her with the overwhelming amount of chores. But something had changed, and there was no way she would open up to him until she knew what he was thinking, especially about her.

"I will go back to my village and bring the healer," Takoda said with real concern in his voice.

"No, you don't have to do that. I think as long as she stays in bed and I keep spoon-feeding her chicken soup, she'll eventually get better." Her words tasted bitter in her mouth. Although what she said was somewhat true, she wasn't sure if Ellie would get better. The word "healer" made Sammie feel uncomfortable. She needed a doctor, not an Indian healer, whatever that was.

"Have you had any visitors this week?" he asked, sitting in the rocker next to her on the porch.

Not knowing that her sister lied about Sammie having a boyfriend, Sammie thought he was talking about the trapper.

"I'm not expecting a visit from anyone with you around," she said, touching his arm. Takoda was unresponsive. Perplexed, she tried another tactic.

"Are we going to ride Gingerbread again?" she asked.

Using his horse to teach her to ride had been an excuse to be with her. Now things were different.

"Yes, but you should try to mount him yourself."

He walked down the ramp and ordered his horse to kneel. When the horse complied, it surprised her. "Now pull your chair up next to the horse and get on. You can do it."

And she did do it. But having only ridden a horse the one time with his help, she was unsure and a little frightened. "I think I still need your help."

"No, you don't; it's time you learned to do this yourself."

Sammie was conflicted. She didn't know if he was trying to help her become more independent, or if he just didn't want to be near her.

"My legs aren't strong enough; I can't hold myself steady on the horse's back."

"Then we will ride another day."

*You don't want to ride with me because of my handicap, do you?* She thought. It was a foolish thought, but his avoidance of close contact made her feel like she repulsed him. Yet before, that didn't seem to be the case. As she settled back into her chair, she was more confused than ever.

"I will go now and bring the healer," Takoda said as he mounted his horse.

"No, you don't need to do that. I know how to treat Ellie." It wasn't that she was so confident in her ability to heal her sister; his lack of affection hurt Sammie, and that made her stubborn.

"I see. You don't trust me, or the healer, do you? As far as you are concerned, I'm just a dumb Indian. Well, our ways are not dumb."

"I know that."

"No, you don't. If you did, you would let us help you."

"That's not it."

"Yes, I think it is. Faith takes more courage than no faith, Sammie. And you have no faith in me, or in God. We all have pain in life, but working through it with God and your friends is easier than doing it without them."

# Chapter Twenty-Six

## Fatherly Advice

The chief sat alone at dusk before a fire outside his hut, smoking a pipe. Takoda came outside and sat across from his father. He waited until his father looked up and acknowledged him before speaking.

"Something troubles you, my son. Tell me, what lies so heavily upon your spirit?"

"I have met the woman I love and wish to court her," Takoda said.

"That is excellent, my son. Which of our lovely Shoshone daughters have you chosen?"

"None, father. I met a white woman on a nearby farm. Her name is Samantha. She is crippled, but it doesn't matter. She can do almost anything."

His father puffed on his pipe a couple of times, blowing out smoke rings as he thought about what his son had just told him. "You must love this woman very much if you can overlook such a problem so quickly. Also, how is she crippled?

"She has never been able to walk, not since birth. She has a chair on wheels, which serves her well in many ways. And, I have watched her leave that chair and work in the fields, pulling herself along the ground planting and harvesting."

"She sounds like a very determined woman who does not allow her limitations to get in the way."

"She is. I have been teaching her to ride Gingerbread. She has learned very quickly, controlling him with just the reins and her words."

"Then what troubles you?"

"I believe another man …a white man is already courting her," Takoda said sadly.

"Ah, I see. Does she love this white man?"

"I don't know. She has never spoken of him, and it seems as though she willingly accepts my intentions towards her. She seems to be very happy whenever I come to the farm. I only found out about him through her younger sister."

"Why then don't you ask the woman herself? I would wonder why she does not speak of him, yet her sister seemed to make a point of telling you. Is the child jealous? How old is she?"

"She is four years younger than Rising Moon."

"I see." The chief puffed again on his pipe, then turning it over, he knocked the tobacco from the pipe's bowl into the fire and stood up. "You are a handsome young brave, my son. It would seem that the younger is trying to create distance between you and Sammie." He smiled kindly at his son.

"How did you know her name? I never told you."

The chief leaned in closer to his eldest, his eyes twinkled. "Do you think your mother and I never talk? She has spent much time at the farm, and she knows you quite well. She is your mother, after all."

"But father, why would Ellie lie to me? I know she likes me."

"Maybe she did, or maybe she is warning you about your competition. Whatever the reason, you would be wise to speak with your mother. She will know what to tell you regarding this white woman you love and her sister. In the meantime, if you are serious, you must ask your sister to make you a courting blanket. And when you court this woman, you must wear your finest clothes and beaded moccasins. Your hair must be carefully groomed. Your sister will help you."

"Did you do all of this when you courted my mother?"

"Yes, I did, and you see the result," his father told him with a grin.

****

The next time Sammie saw him, Takoda was riding over the hill, but he wasn't alone. An Indian girl rode beside him on another painted horse. As they raced along the ridge of the mountain above the farm, Sammie could hear them laughing.

Sammie was hurt. Once they were out of sight, she looked down at her wheelchair; the reason he was never coming back.

****

# Chapter Twenty-Seven

## A Visit from the Healer

The next afternoon, Takoda returned to the farm. Sammie was really glad to see him even though their relationship was strained. She found herself unable to hide her smile as he climbed off his horse.

"Good afternoon," Sammie said, continuing to smile.

"Good afternoon to you, too," Takoda said, returning a smile.

"I brought the healer with me."

Sammie looked around, but she didn't see anyone.

"The Healer is waiting in the trees for you to permit them to see Ellie."

Sammie had thought about his offer at length. What did she have to lose? Ellie wasn't getting better, and nothing she had done had helped. Why not an Indian healer? She would keep a close eye on this medicine man and not let him do anything to hurt Ellie.

"Yes, please."

Takoda turned and waved to the trees. She was expecting to see a skinny old man covered in feathers and face paint, walk out of the forest. What she saw was a strikingly beautiful, white woman with hair, the color of freshly picked corn, worn in a single thick braid. She looked to be in her early forties, was rather petite, and rode bareback on a fawn-colored horse. Dressed in typical Indian garb and guiding her horse out of the forest and down the hill, the Healer approached the cabin and Sammie with a warm smile.

"You must be Sammie. I have heard much about you."

She dismounted from her horse gracefully and walked up the ramp to where Sammie sat in her wheelchair. Sammie couldn't have been more surprised.

"You were expecting an Indian, perhaps even a man?

"To tell you the truth, yes."

The woman gave Sammie a sincere hug.

"My given name is Rachel. My Indian name translates to Beautiful Moon. It's very nice to meet you, at last, Samantha. I know you must be confused, and I will explain everything to you. But I understand you have a sister who is ill. Why don't you take me to her, and we can talk after I examine her."

"Of course, thank you."

"Takoda, please bring my medicine bag."

Her son grabbed a leather bag from her horse and followed his mother inside. Sammie followed in her chair.

"I've been so worried. I tried to do everything I could think of. She seems to get better for a short time, and then she gets worse."

They entered the bedroom and found Ellie sleeping fitfully.

"I'll do my best. I've bought some herbs and medicine. I think it will help. The advantage of being a white woman and living as an Indian is that I know both worlds."

Rachel walked up to the bed and laid a soft hand on Ellie's forehead. The movement woke the sick girl.

"Hello, Ellie. My name is Rachel. I came to see if I can help you feel better and to pray with you."

Ellie looked at her sister, who was standing on the other side of the bed.

"It's alright," Sammie assured her.

The healer pulled a stethoscope out of her bag and listened to Ellie's lungs.

Sammie, shocked, blurted out, "A stethoscope! Where did you get that? I've wanted one for the longest time, as I have studied everything I can about medicine, but Pa said they were sold only to doctors."

"That is true. However, my father was a doctor, so I inherited his when he died, along with a few other medical instruments."

"Your father was a doctor? Then why…"

"I promise, Sammie, as soon as I finish up with Ellie, I'll answer all your questions."

Sammie blushed over her impatience. "I'm sorry. Please go ahead…."

After her examination, Rachel used herbs and salves to treat Ellie. Then she took a bottle of medicine containing a mixture of swamp cabbage root mixed with honey.

"This is a medicine made especially for whooping cough," Rachel explained to both girls. "Take a spoonful of this three times a day and through the night…every eight hours."

Sammie brought her a spoon. When the healer poured out a spoonful, Ellie wrinkled her nose.

"I can't take that. It smells awful!"

"I know, dear, and I'm sorry. Unfortunately, another name for swamp cabbage root is skunk root because of the smell. The honey helps with the taste. Just hold your nose and swallow it down."

Ellie shot a pleading look at Sammie.

"I know, sweetie, but if it's the best thing available to help with your whooping cough, please take it, and I'll give you some fruit to take away the taste."

Ellie did as she was told, and when the medicine entered her mouth, she gagged, but then she swallowed it, making an awful face. She shivered in revulsion.

Rachel gently wiped the sweat from Ellie's face and laid a cold cloth on her forehead. She then laid hands on her.

"Dear Father, heal this beautiful little girl that she may spend her days bringing you the glory that you deserve. Take this sickness from her. I pray this in Jesus' name. Amen."

Moments after the prayer, Ellie fell asleep.

Rachel and Sammie went out on the porch so that Ellie would not be disturbed. The healer sat comfortably in one of the rocking chairs. "I do miss rocking chairs," she said, gently giving herself a little push. Sammie placed her wheelchair across from her. Takoda went to the kitchen to make tea from some of the herbs his mother brought.

"Samantha, I'm leaving this salve for you to rub on Ellie's neck and chest. Once in the morning and also once at night. She needs lots of rest, plenty of water, and the medicine as prescribed. Make sure you give it to her every eight hours. That will help. These herbs should be boiled into a tea and given to her in addition to the water. Her condition is serious."

When the tea was ready, Takoda gave the two women each a cup. Then he pulled the other rocker up next to the healer.

"How did you become the tribe's healer?" Sammie asked.

"I was fourteen when my father, who was a doctor in Boston, believed that God wanted him, well our family, to move out of the city and head west to join a wagon train. I remember him saying, 'There are plenty of doctors and preachers in Boston. Let's go where there are none.' He wanted to bring modern medicine and God's story to the people moving and settling in the West – the pioneers. My mother shared his vision and passion. I guess you could call them missionaries."

"My father was a banker in New York, but he had always wanted to become a farmer. That's why we're here. I like living on a farm, but Ellie hates it."

"I wasn't happy either, at first. My dream was to follow in my father's footsteps and become a doctor. I believed that would never happen if we moved out of Boston. I was angry when we left, but once we joined the wagon train and became part of that community, I started to care for the people. Also, because my father was the only doctor, I was able to assist him whenever he was needed. Father brought all his medical books with him, and I regularly read on the long journey. I was learning and working alongside my father, and it seemed maybe moving west would work after all.

"But when we came through the pass not far from here," she continued, "Indians attacked us. Many of the people in our wagon train were killed, including my mother and sister. Father was badly injured. I cared for him for two days until a small scouting party came upon us. At first, I had thought they had come to finish us off, but then I realized that they weren't the ones who had attacked us. This group was compassionate, and they took all the survivors back to their village."

"So, they took you?" Sammie asked.

"Yes. When I showed them the medical bag and books, they allowed me to bring them and supplies back to their village. Unfortunately, my father's injuries were too severe. We had two more days together before he died. During that time, he told me not to be bitter, but to forgive those who'd harmed us, to learn from the people who had so generously saved the survivors, and to tell them about Jesus."

Sammie was gripped by the story. How could her father have asked her to forgive the very people that had killed most of his family? Rachel sipped her tea and continued. "A few weeks later, I turned fifteen, marriageable age. The men in the village argued with the Chief over who should have me. Thankfully, the Chief was kind, and waited, knowing that I still grieved for my parents. For eighteen months, I lived with a squaw and her children. She was the tribe's healer. As I learned their language, she discovered a little English. We compared our healing techniques. Onatah taught me, and I showed her.

"My father's medical books were my most prized possession. The only thing more important is my faith, my trust in God, and my spiritual journey."

"I wanted to become a doctor, as well," Sammie replied. "And my Pa purchased as many medical books for me as we could fit into our wagon. They, too, are my most prized possessions."

Rachel smiled knowingly. "At seventeen, I married the Chief. We didn't expect to, but we fell in love. His kindness, fairness, and leadership were traits I admired. When I explained to him about Jesus, he understood and prayed for Jesus to lead him and his tribe. He is fifteen years older than me. His first wife died from typhoid. I believe that God chose him for me. He is a good man – kind, brave, and funny. Our son," she smiled at Takoda, "Is very much like his father."

Rachel looked over at Takoda.

"She's your ma?"

"Yes, this is my mother, my English American mother. See," he pointed to his face and wiggled his eyebrows, "We have the same eyes." The three of them laughed. "I wanted you to meet her, from that first day we met, and now you have. But we must return to the village. There are many tasks to finish before the sun sets."

Rachel stood up and leaned over, hugged Sammie. The two immediately formed a bond.

"Take care of your sister," Rachel said.

Takoda helped his mother place her bags on her horse. He adored her, and Sammie admired that about him.

As Sammie watched them ride off. She hoped that Takoda would look back and wave just like he used to. He didn't. Sammie went inside and checked on Ellie, who was still sleeping. Then she rolled back into the living room and picked up her mother's Bible. She settled into one of the chairs in the living room and began to read. This time the words seemed to make more sense. She wondered at the strength and love that came from Takoda's mother, and she realized how much she was like her own mother. Could their faith be the same? Reading from a part of the Bible called 'John,' she began to understand.

# Chapter Twenty-Eight

## Prayers and Truths

Sammie had just finished the morning chores when leaving the barn. She noticed Rachel riding across the field. Sammie immediately looked to see if Takoda was with her. He wasn't, and Sammie was hurt that he had not visited for the past week.

Rebecca dismounted and removed a couple of bundles from her horse. Sammie wanted to ask her how Takoda was but was too embarrassed to ask. She acted like she hadn't thought of him every moment of every day.

"Good morning, Sammie," Rachel called out to her.

"Good morning to you, Mrs. Rachel."

Rebecca had told Sammie to call her by her first name, but Sammie's parents had taught her if she was going to call an adult by their first name; she should put 'Mr., Mrs., or Miss' before their name.

"How was your ride?" Sammie asked.

"Any ride through God's wonderful creation is wonderful. How is Ellie doing today?"

"She had a rough night. She has a dry hacking cough and is finding it difficult to breathe. A couple of times she was gasping so hard for air that it scared me half to death."

Rachel frowned. "I've brought along more medicine. I'm sorry it was such a hard night."

"It's just that I'm so afraid. I'm trying to be brave, but it's hard. My brother died from this. I remember everything and Ellie. I couldn't bear to lose her, too."

Rachel moved to Sammie, bent over, and embraced the frightened young woman, allowing her to cry softly in her arms. *Poor thing*, Rachel thought. *Here she is all alone with a sick sister, and who knows when her parents will return.* As she held Sammie, she silently petitioned to God, *Father, help, please. Heal Ellie, Lord Jesus. Show your mercy and love to these two girls, who are so alone. Give them faith and encourage them, Father. Protect them. Thank you.*

Rachel felt Sammie take a deep breath. She pulled away as the girl wiped her tears and smiled up at her.

"Thank you."

"Sometimes, we need to cry. And that's alright, but we also need to pray that Ellie gets better. Pray for God to heal her."

Sammie had questions about prayer but, for now, keeping them to herself.

Rachel followed Sammie into the cabin and then to the bedroom. Ellie was lying on top of all the blankets, her nightshirt soaking wet. She had lost almost ten pounds from not eating and looked gaunt and exhausted from coughing.

"How are you feeling, sweetheart?"

When Ellie tried to answer, she only coughed, her eyes streaming tears.

Rachel placed her hand on Ellie's forehead and looked at Sammie.

"She's still running a high temperature."

"I spent most of the night putting wet towels on her body," Sammie said.

"That was good. You probably kept Ellie's fever from going even higher. But I'm concerned about you. Staying up all night and working so hard during the day is going to make you sick, too."

"She's my sister. I have to do everything I can for her."

"Together, Sammie, with God's help and my medicine, we'll pray, and together we will believe that she will get well. Now, I want you to rest. Go ahead, take this blanket, and lay on the sofa. I'll watch over Ellie. You need some sleep. Go on."

Sammie knew she was right. She was so worried about Ellie, but if she got sick too, that would be terrible. They might both die. *Stop that, Samantha McPherson! You are not going to think the worse. Concentrate on the moment, on Ellie getting better. Trust Rachel trust God.*

Five hours later, Sammie awoke to a wonderful smell from the large pot over the fire. Rebecca was in the kitchen. There were clean clothes folded on a chair, and the house looked like it had been dusted and cleaned.

"You slept well, Sammie. That's good. Ellie seems to be doing better. Supper is in the pot, and I made some tortillas for you. I hope you like them. "

Sammie was so grateful, and she felt so much better, like she could handle another night, another day. She saw that Rachel had done most of the inside chores and thanked her. Rachel had some of Sammie's medical books out on the table, and together they discussed different treatments and medical procedures. All the while, Ellie slept; her breathing was not as labored as it had been.

As evening approached, and Rachel prepared to leave, Sammie couldn't stand it any longer.

"How is Takoda," she asked.

"He's fine, Sammie. He is very upset over a broken relationship, but he will recover."

Sammie wanted to ask if he was sad over their relationship, or with the Indian girl she had seen with him on the mountain ridge. However, she was too embarrassed to say anything.

"You look like you want to ask something, Sammie."

"Nothing. Just. Well, thank you. Thank you for everything today. And have a safe ride back. You will be home before dark, won't you?"

"Oh, yes. If I leave now, Kiki is swift. Besides, she wants to get home to her supper."

Rachel hugged Sammie before she climbed on her horse and felt Sammie's lingering strong embrace. She looked into the young woman's eyes and realized Sammie didn't want her to go. Her heart went out to her.

"Next time I visit, would you like me to stay a couple of nights to allow you to sleep?"

"No, I'm fine. But thank you for asking."

*She is brave,* thought Rachel, determined in her heart to come back sooner.

As she turned her horse and rode away, Rachel gave Sammie a gracious smile. Once Rachel was out of sight, Sammie started crying.

Ellie heard her sister cry and felt terrible. She knew Sammie was working hard without her help. She also knew how much Sammie missed Takoda, and she began to feel guilty about lying to him. She wanted to say something, to tell her sister the truth, but it was such a terrible lie. Sammie would never forgive her. Her guilt, more than her illness, kept Ellie awake long into the night, as the lie continued to eat her up inside.

****

Rachel came back the next day and continued to visit every day. And every day Sammie would look for Takoda, riding Gingerbread next to her, only to be disappointed that he hadn't come. *What did I do? What did I say?* She went over and over their last conversation in detail, and every time it came back to her legs, and being less than other women. *I guess I was a novelty at first, and then he realized what it would really be like to be with me and not be able to ride away, back to his normal life.* She wanted to hate him for that, but she couldn't. She just couldn't. Instead, her heart ached every time she thought of him.

Rachel would spend the day taking care of Ellie, while Sammie did the chores. Ellie began to get better, which allowed the two to talk, play table games, and read together. Sammie was so thankful that her sister was getting better; she did her work with renewed energy and joy.

At the end of each visit, Rachel would tell Ellie a Bible story, and she looked forward to this particular time and was impressed by how well Takoda's mother knew the Bible. Rachel was as kind and loving as her ma. She knew it was because they both lived and acted like the Bible said they should. She thought that was how she wanted to be, like her ma and Rachel, and the wonderful women heroines in the Bible. Her favorite story was Esther. Ellie would often act out in her mind how she would have handled her husband, the king, and the evil Haman. She thought about how brave Esther was, which finally made her speak up.

"Can I tell you something I need to say out loud," Ellie asked.

"Of course, little one."

"Will you hate me?"

"No."

"No matter what?"

"No matter what, sweetheart, I could never hate you."

"I told your son a lie," Ellie admitted.

"What kind of lie?"

"I told him my sister had a suitor…a beau. She doesn't."

Rachel was quiet for a few moments, then responded to Ellie's confession, "That explains why he had so hurt a few days ago when he came back from here."

Ellie just sat in bed, not knowing what to say. There was a very long silence, and then Rachel looked quizzically at the young girl.

"Why did you lie, Ellie?"

"I was jealous that Sammie was happy, and Takoda was making her happy. I didn't want her to be happy if I couldn't be happy."

"And what about Takoda?"

"I didn't even think of him or his feelings," she said sadly.

"Lying does that. It always hurts more people than we think."

"I'm so sorry," Ellie said genuinely.

"You don't need to apologize to me, Ellie, but I do think there are two other people that need to hear from you."

"I know. But now I'm too embarrassed and ashamed."

"Yes, I would imagine you are. But that doesn't change what you know you should do. I think Takoda deserves to hear the truth, and so does your sister. Don't let embarrassment stop you from doing the right thing."

And with those words, she kissed Ellie on her forehead and left for the day.

*****

That evening when Sammie came in from chores, Ellie called her into the bedroom. Exhausted, but happy that her sister was feeling so much better, Sammie rolled her chair next to the bed.

Ellie hesitated for several moments, coughed, and then blurted out. "I lied to Takoda and told him you had a male caller who was courting you."

"You what? Why would you do that?"

Ellie hung her head. "I liked him, and I was jealous because he liked you."

"Ellie, he likes us both,"

"You know what I mean."

"You think he likes me? Likes me like that?"

"Can't you see it in his eyes and how he acts around you? I mean look, he stacked all that wood and brought you flowers every day, did chores, caught us a fish, had dinner with us.

"He did that for us."

"He did that for *you,* Sammie. He taught *you* how to ride a horse."

Sammie's head spun as she thought about the last few weeks. She had felt that Takoda's coldness and distance was because of her handicap. Now she knew it wasn't.

"Sammie, I'm so sorry."

Sammie held out her arms to her sister, and Ellie leaned out of her bed, and they hugged each other tightly.

"Thank you for being brave enough to tell me you lied," Sammie told her.

"Will you forgive me?

"Yes." Sammie was so excited to learn the real reason Takoda had been avoiding her. It was easy to forgive her sister.

"But please tell me what did you ever say to Takoda that made him believe I had a suitor? We haven't seen a boy, man, or scarecrow around here for months…except that old trapper. Oh my, you didn't tell him it was the trapper, did you?"

"Of course not, I made something up. You know how good an *actress* I am. I told him your beau hadn't been around because he had to go to the big city to buy you a ring."

"Ellie! That's…well…." Sammie started to laugh. "That's just preposterous!"

"He believed me."

"Someone is going to have to tell him the truth." Sammie widened her eyes and poked her sister lovingly in the ribs.

"I know. I will. Promise."

"That is a promise I will make sure you keep. Now let's have some dinner. Think you can eat at the table tonight?"

"Yes!"

# Chapter Twenty-Nine

## Forgive and Forget

The next day when Rachel arrived, Takoda followed on Gingerbread. Sammie couldn't hide the smile on her face, and neither could he.

"Before you two talk, I need to take Takoda in to see Ellie," Rachel said.

Sammie stayed outside, not wanting her sister to be more embarrassed than she already would be. The other two walked into the cabin. From the porch, she wouldn't hear the three talking.

A few minutes later, Takoda came out on the porch.

"Your sister told me the truth. I want you to know that I am sorry, Sammie. I should have spoken to you about my disappointment instead of running away like a coward."

"I was so miserable, wondering what I had done wrong, or worse, that you couldn't bear the sight of me anymore."

"From now on, if something seems wrong, or just not right, I promise to talk it over with you first. This way, there will be no misunderstandings between us."

Sammie flashed him a beautiful smile. "And I promise to do the same. But can I ask you one question?"

"Yes."

"Who was that beautiful Indian girl you were riding with on the ridge?"

Takoda was starting to laugh, "That was my *sister*. I will share your compliment with her."

That afternoon Sammie and Takoda worked together outside the entire day. At one point, Takoda stopped and stared at Sammie. He couldn't help it.

Sammie noticed him and said, "You're staring."

"I can't help it. I have watched you for so many weeks, first from the hillside and now right here next to you. Your beauty and bravery take me. You remind me of a White Dove."

"White Dove? Is that my Indian name?" Sammie asked, smiling shyly.

"Yes. White Dove is the name I have chosen for you."

"I like it. I only wish I could fly like one," she said wistfully.

"Ah, but perhaps you will." Takoda placed several stalks of corn in the basket and straightened to his full height. Sammie realized how very tall he was.

"Mother has done some research in her medical books. She has some questions she must ask you first, but she said it might be possible, with a lot of work, for you to learn how to move your legs, and maybe, just maybe, learn how to walk someday."

Sammie's eyes lit up. "To walk? On these two legs? But how...?"

"Ah, White Dove." He knelt next to her and placed his two hands over hers, overtaken with her innocence and hope. "Your eyes are as blue as the early evening sky just before the sun starts to set. And they light up when you are happy."

"Thank you," she blushed at the compliment and warmth of his large hands covering hers.

"I believe I want you to walk as much as you do. But, if you never take a step, what I feel for you in my heart will never change."

Sammie caught her breath. *His heart? Did he say what he feels in his heart?* She stared at him, feeling her heartbeat skip.

The Indian boy gently laid his hand on her cheek and continued, "I don't know all the details; my mother will explain. She has some questions that may be difficult to ask, and she doesn't want to hurt your feelings. But I believe in my mother's gift of healing. I have seen her work. And I know she will do everything to help you. We both will." Sammie again found it difficult to breathe, just thinking about the possibility that she may one day walk.

Takoda squeezed her hand, then stood again and surveyed the work they had accomplished. "I have something I must do. Will you be alright here by yourself?"

Sammie looked at him questioningly, but since he had been working side-by-side with her all day, she didn't want to ask where he was going. *It's not my place,* she thought. Instead, she patted her trusty rifle and smiled.

"Don't worry. Me and old Betsy will be fine."

"I won't be gone long, and I'll be close enough to hear if you need to yell for help. I promise."

Sammie nodded, and Takoda took off at a run. Returning to the stalks of corn, she continued picking the ripe ones and thought, *I wonder where he went. Is there something the tribe needs him for?* She pushed aside her thoughts and concentrated on the corn. Time seemed to fly, and before she knew it, Takoda stood before her with a big smile.

"This will make a fine dinner for the four of us," he said, pulling a large fish from behind his back. Then he frowned slightly. "Do you know how to cook fish?" Teasing her with the same question, he had asked the first time he brought them a fish. At the questioning look on her face, he said, "After all, I did fry up the last batch."

"Really, Takoda, I make a delicious fish stew with potatoes, onions, greens, and a mixture of spices. The recipe is a family secret that I will take to my deathbed," she teased as she reached for the giant fish.

"It's a trout," Takoda said, holding it out of her reach. "We can always roast it over an open fire."

"Oh? Well, if you'll prepare the fire, you can roast it if you like. After all, you caught it." Her eyes sparkled with mischief.

"Hmmm." Takoda held the fish close to inspect it. "Now that I think about it, I did *catch* it. So it's only fair that *you* should cook it." He smiled and, with a slight bow, placed it in her arms.

Sammie was startled by a most pleasant feeling, as Takoda's hand touched her arm. She hoped he hadn't noticed the involuntary shiver. She found herself smiling up at the Indian boy, keenly aware of how very handsome he was. Sammie's heartbeat an extra beat. *What was this?* She was afraid to even think about it.

"I accept your challenge, Takoda."

He quickly stepped behind the wheelchair and turned her toward the cabin door. Bending at the waist, he whispered into her ear. "It seems your arms are full. Allow me."

His breath on her ear made her heartbeat even faster and with every turn of the wheels, faster still. He steered her toward the kitchen, and what would prove to be the first fun and relaxing evening she had experienced since the last one they had weeks ago.

# Chapter Thirty

## The Water Rises

They had been on the road for nearly a week when Ben and his wife came to the swollen river. The obstacle was just a day and a half away from the farm. The roads they'd been on had been muddy and rough due to all the rain that had fallen over the past several days. But both were anxious to get home. They'd been gone far longer than they had anticipated. They hoped at least one of their messages had reached the girls through other travelers, but they couldn't be sure. Ellen especially couldn't wait to wrap the girls in her arms. She had missed them terribly and prayed for them earnestly. She knew it in her heart they were alright, but she had to see for herself and hold them close. The sight of the swollen, fast-moving river crushed their spirit.

"What are we going to do?" Ellen asked Ben. "We can't possibly cross that river. Look, it's up over the banks."

Both sides of the road leading into the river were filled with wagons and people on horseback. A few had braved the raging waters and made it across. Others turned around after going only a short distance.

Ben was impatient. He wanted to get to the farm. He hadn't forgotten about Dugger or his suspicions about the man. He never said anything to Ellen about his distrust of the trapper but kept his thoughts to himself. The sooner they got home to their daughters, the better.

The rain had finally stopped in the middle of the night on their first day there, so they waited three days, spending the next two watching the water recede. It seemed to take forever.

"I can't wait any longer. We need to get home," Ben said on day four.

"Are you sure we can make it?" Ellen asked worriedly.

"The water is lower than before. Look," he said, pointing, "It isn't overlapping the banks anymore. I say we give it a try."

His wife nodded. "As long as you think it's safe. Just remember, I don't swim very well. And I'm still not very strong."

"Just stay in the wagon and hang on, Ellen. You'll be fine. The current doesn't look that bad. Yesterday two larger wagons got across."

Using the reins, Ben urged the horses forward at a slow pace. Others decided to join them. One covered wagon washed away almost immediately. Ellen held tightly to the rim of the wagon. She didn't say a word, only watched as two of the occupants swam to shore. She didn't see the other two and lost sight of it as they rounded the bend. Still, others seemed to be doing fine. They were halfway across, and Ben was feeling good about his decision when one of the horses lost his footing, the other horse followed, and they were soon being swept downriver.

"Hang on, Ellen, hang on tight," Ben yelled over the rushing water and screaming horses. But even he couldn't hang on and felt himself slide off to the side, almost going under the muddy water. With sheer determination, he pulled himself back onto the wagon and tried to crawl back to his terrified wife. The back of the wagon was quickly filling with water as it rocked from side to side.

"Leave me," Ellen urged her husband. "I'm not strong enough yet to swim, especially with this corset."

"No, we can make it. Hang on!" He shouted above the roar of the rushing water. They, too, were swept around the bend in the river.

Back at the crossing, Dugger sat on his stolen horse and watched as the McPherson's wagon and others were swept away.

"Too bad," he said aloud.

"What's that, Dugger," a friend of his asked.

"The wagons caught by the current. Ya see em disappear around the bend there? No doubt, everyone drowned."

"No doubt."

Inwardly, Dugger smiled. *Looks like Little Sister and her sibling are on their own for good. Guess I'll have to stop by and lend em' a hand.*

*****

The next day, Sammie woke slowly in a fog. Then she turned over and went right back to her dream:

*She sat on a huge front porch of a beautiful little cabin, at least three times larger than their current front porch. Four cows were lined up in front of the porch, and the chickens were milking the cows. It didn't seem strange at all as the chickens talked amongst themselves about everyday matters. Ellie stood on the back of a bright red wooden wagon, singing. She was dressed in a purple chiffon dress that reached her toes and wore a wide-brimmed purple hat. The wagon ran around and around the yard by itself, and Ellie never stopped singing, nor lost her footing.*

*Sammie enjoyed this so much. It seemed like a perfectly wonderful morning. Then the door opened, and twin girls—toddlers with foppish brown hair and cherubic faces* ran from inside, followed by a pig dressed in the same purple gown as Ellie. Two older boys followed. They were perhaps six and seven years old, looking very much like the two little girls, laughing and jumping around the pig.

"My, thought Sammie, "everyone seems so happy. I wonder who they are." She looked down at her lap and discovered she was knitting. She wasn't sure what it was at first, but suddenly it jumped out of her lap and ran off the porch toward the barn. It was a multi-colored long-haired collie. She laughed as he knitted collie ran circles around her and barked, "Thank you, thank you, thank you."

"What a gifted knitter I must be to have created such a colorful dog," she thought.

Then Takoda rode into the front yard on a beautiful two-headed horse. He waved at her and held up yet another small child, actually just a baby.

"Sammie, look! I've brought you another little girl!"

He quickly jumped off his horse and bringing the baby to Sammie, gently laid it in her lap. "Let's name her Monkey Face," he said with delight.

"Oh, no! She's too beautiful, Takoda." She looked at the tiny infant, smiling up at her. "Let's name her Sunrise."

"Yes. Perfect." He leaned over and kissed Sammie. Then he jumped into the red wagon with Ellie, joining her in song.

Sammie awoke with a start, sat up, and touched her cheek. Then she snuggled back under the covers and thought about her dream.

\*\*\*\*

Around mid-morning, Rachel rode up and found Sammie sitting on the porch, snapping the ends off green beans, breaking them in thirds, and tossing them into a tub of water. She planned on canning them today.

"Good morning," Sammie called. "I haven't seen you for a while. I've missed you!" Sammie saw the large satchel Rachel had with her. "Does this mean I get a weaving lesson today?"

"Good morning," Rachel replied. "And yes, you get a weaving lesson." She slid gracefully from her horse and stepped onto the porch. "But there's something else too. I hope I'm not crossing a boundary here. I want to talk to you about something. If you think it's none of my business, then please tell me if you'd rather not discuss it."

Her words made Sammie curious. "What could you possibly want to talk about that you think would offend me?"

"Your legs. What happened, and how did you end up in a wheelchair?" Rachel sat in her favorite porch rocker and pulled it closer to Sammie.

Sammie remembered the conversation with Takoda, and that his mother had been doing research in her medical books about her crippled legs. She replied to Rachel with gratitude for bringing up the subject.

"I don't mind talking about it. It's who I am. My parents told me I never crawled, and the doctors told them I was born that way and would never walk. At first, they carried me around. But as I grew older, I became too heavy. So they had a small wheelchair made for me. This is my third chair. I received it just before we left New York." She laughed and spun the chair in a circle, making Takoda's mother smile. "It is most definitely the best one I've ever had."

"You are a remarkable young woman, Sammie. Do you mind if I look at and touch your legs?"

"I guess not." She pulled up her skirt and bared her thin legs to Rachel.

"I've been studying my medical books, and I don't know how crippled you are, or if there could be an improvement. If I look at your legs, perhaps I could understand better what caused this. Maybe we can strengthen these muscles." She reached out and felt the calves and then the thigh muscles of Sammie's legs.

"Hmm," she said thoughtfully. "Let me show you something." She reached into her pouch and pulled out a thick, well-worn book. "This was my father's, and as you know, he was a doctor in Boston. I did a little studying. Look at this." With her index finger, Rachel pointed to a drawing and some paragraphs written next to it. "I know you won't understand this at first, but Sammie, I think you may have enough good muscles to build up some strength. Would you be willing to give it a try?"

"Yes, of course! Do you really think I might be able to walk?"

"I cannot say for sure, but we won't know until we try. If nothing else, I believe it would help you get in and out of bed or a chair easier. And when you're on the floor, you may be able to use your legs to pull yourself around, maybe even crawl, but I can't make any promises. It will be hard work and will sometimes hurt."

"I don't care. If I could just walk even a little bit, it would be wonderful! And if all I can do is crawl, it will still make my life easier." Sammie could hardly contain her excitement. Walking was an ongoing dream her parents had tried to discourage, not wanting to get her hopes up.

Yet Takoda's mother thought she might have a chance. If so, it would be the greatest gift she had ever received. She looked up toward heaven. *Thank You, Lord, for giving me this chance. If you can help me walk, you will be answering not only my own prayers but my mother's as well.*

"All right, I'll come every day and work your calves. And I'll teach you exercises you can do by yourself as much as you like. I think your thigh muscles are fine, but we need to see if we can strengthen these muscles right here." She lightly touched both calves. "Would you like to start now?"

"Yes!"

Rachel wheeled her into the cabin and reached into her large pouch, pulling out a thick yellowish salve. She rubbed it into her hands and then gently began to massage Sammie's right calf. Sammie reacted with a little gasp. She was surprised she could feel the pressure, and it hurt a little as Takoda's mother increased the kneading of her leg. For more than an hour, Rachel's strong hands lovingly massaged the girl's calves until both she and Sammie were quite tired.

"That's good for today. Tomorrow, I'll bring more salve and show you how to do this. Then we'll start on the other things we can do to help regain some movement and strength in your legs."

Sammie looked at her with tears in her eyes. "Thank you, Rachel. Thank you for trying to help me."

"There's one more thing. Let's ask God to heal your legs. I don't know what His answer will be, Sammie, but He says that we can ask Him for anything, and healing is one of his specialties."

Sammie closed her eyes and felt Rachel reach out and touch the back of her legs.

"Dear Father of heaven and earth, we come to you with a humble request. We ask that you restore the strength to Sammie's legs. We know that you have the power to do this right now, immediately, if you want to. Or you can use the methods you have taught us. Her desire, dear Father, is to walk. If this is in your plan for this daughter of yours, please do this for her. We ask this in the name of your son, the one who has brought us new life for eternity. Amen."

Sammie felt warmth throughout her whole body. Would God heal her? She looked at Rachel as she stood up. With a beautiful, graceful movement, she leaned over and kissed Sammie on the forehead. It felt like an angel had kissed her.

"Have faith, Sammie. God will answer our prayer. We don't know *how* or *when,* but it will always be what is best for you."

With a wave, she walked through the door. Sammie was left to think about the words Rachel had said. And for the first time in her life, hope that someday she might walk, filled her with peace. She didn't want to get her hopes too high. But finally, she believed she at least had a chance.

Sammie dreamt that night of running - chasing Takoda. Then just before she reached him, he flew off into the sky, never looking back.

# Chapter Thirty-One

## Tidings of War

Sammie's physical therapy continued daily, with more and more things added to increase her chances of strengthening her leg muscles. Now when she rode Gingerbread by herself, she discovered that she was able to squeeze her legs enough to help control him. Then, another exercise was added to her daily routine.

"Today, we will begin your swimming lessons," Takoda announced after lunch.

"What? Swimming? I don't know. I'm afraid of the lake."

"Do not worry, White Dove. I will hold you steady in the water as you do your exercises."

"But…"

"My mother says you must learn to push beyond your wheelchair. Now that you are gaining more strength with your legs, you must use them as much as you can."

Sammie looked at his face, his expression so earnest, his eyes so filled with love.

"Do you trust me?"

She laughed. "I've heard those words before."

He grinned. "And I have kept my word, have I not?"

"Yes, you have. I'll change into my bathing costume."

It didn't take her long, and soon they were on Gingerbread headed for the lake. Takoda allowed her to guide the horse.

"You are controlling the horse more and more with your legs, instead of just the reins. I am very proud of how dedicated you are and the progress you have made so far."

Sammie smiled. "You can tell the difference?"

"Can't you?"

She looked down for a moment.

"You must allow yourself to believe in your accomplishments. Every little bit of progress you make takes you that much closer to freedom and independence."

She looked up and grinned. "You're right."

"Of course, I am!"

Sammie burst out laughing. " 'Of course,' huh? Well, see how you like this!" With a shout of joy, she pressed her knees into Gingerbread, signaling him to gallop.

Takoda gave a real Indian cry as his horse took off running. He remembered the timid girl he had placed on Gingerbread for the first time and realized that she no longer existed. She now rode a horse as well as any woman in his tribe. Takoda was very proud of her.

Jumping from Gingerbread's back, he pulled her off, both of them laughing as he held her upright in his arms. Suddenly the laughter stopped, and they found themselves gazing into each other's eyes. Time seemed to stand still as they lost themselves to the moment. Then he kissed her tenderly. Sammie kissed him back and sighed as she laid her head against his chest.

"I wish moments like these would never end," she said.

"Hmm, I agree."

A crow began to squawk, ruining the moment.

"Sit here," he said as he lowered her to the grass and removed his shirt.

Sammie looked at his lean muscled chest and blushed. *He's so strong,* she thought.

Then he scooped her up into his arms and carried her into the water.

"Oh!" Sammie cried as the cold water hit her back and legs. "It's so cold!"

"You will warm up," Takoda assured her. "Especially once you start your exercises. And you know what else?"

"What?" she asked.

"Although moving though water is easier, it uses more energy as you push against the current. Better exercise for your muscles." He lowered her until the water was chest high.

"Wait! What are you doing?" Sammie asked in a panic.

"You must learn to relax. Struggling and thrashing around will cause you to go beneath the surface."

"But…."

"No buts. Concentrate on relaxing, starting with your feet, and work up to the top of your head."

"Don't let go of me!" She tried to relax as he instructed. "Like this?" she asked a moment later. She sounded calmer.

"That's it. Now, allow the tension to flow down your body and out the ends of your toes. Trust me; remember, I will not allow you to drown."

It took some effort, but Sammie slowly did as he told her until she was floating in the water.

"You're floating all by yourself," Takoda declared with a smile.

"What? Am I …floating? Without your help?"

"You are," he replied, showing her his hands.

"Wait! Your hands…."

Sammie tensed up and began to sink. Takoda caught her just after her face wholly submerged. She came up coughing and choking on water. As soon as she stopped, she hit him in the shoulder.

"You promised you wouldn't let me drown!" She raised her fist to hit him again.

"If you hit me again, I will drop you."

Sammie's fist sank back to the water.

"I didn't let you drown. You panicked and tried to drown yourself."

"But…"

"But nothing, relax and believe in yourself."

Knowing what he said was true, she started the process once more and was soon floating. After a moment or two, she said, "You can let go now."

"I already have," Takoda said, showing his hands once more.

He let her float for awhile.

"This is nice," she finally admitted. "But I don't see how this is helping me exercise my legs."

"It isn't, but if a situation ever arises where you fall into the water, floating may just keep you alive. Now, part two is where the exercise begins. I want you to start kicking your legs. We can start with you on your back, and then later; you'll flip over and kick. If your kick becomes strong enough, you'll be on your way to learning to swim.

They spent thirty minutes at it. Sammie's kicks were feeble at best, barely moving her legs, but Takoda encouraged her to keep at it.

"You'll get stronger, as long as you keep working at it," he assured her. "Remember how much effort it took to learn how to use your thighs to ride Gingerbread?"

Sammie slowly nodded.

"But, you conquered it, and you will do the same with this."

When they arrived back at the cabin, Takoda helped her from her horse to her wheelchair. "Wait right here. I have a surprise for you."

Takoda headed for the barn, while Sammie thought about all she had accomplished since starting her physical therapy. She was lost in thought over her progress that she forgot about her surprise. That is until he stood in front of her holding a pair of crutches.

Sammie's eyes went wide. "Where did you get those?"

"My mother showed me a picture in one of her medical books. Since you and she are about the same height, I made them using her to judge how long they should be. I can't wait until you are strong enough to try them out."

Sammie looked at him with anticipation.

"No, not yet, you have to develop a lot more strength in your lower legs first, but I thought this would be a good goal to encourage you."

"You made these? Oh, Takoda, they're so beautiful."

"Really?"

"Now look who's underestimating himself. They are very nicely made; you did a wonderful job, but it's what they represent that makes them so wonderful. When I reach a point when I can use them, it means I'll be walking! Truly walking!"

Sammie was about to say something else when a brave rode up, his horse breathing heavily from running so fast.

"Liwanu, what has happened?" Takoda asked. His expression was one of concern. Out of respect for Sammie, the young brave spoke to Takoda in broken English.

"Comanche tribe on the warpath. Attack many homesteads and invade our land," Liwanu replied.

"Comanches?" Sammie asked Takoda. "What is your tribe?"

"Our tribe is Shoshone. The Comanches have been making war across the area the white man calls Colorado for years," Takoda replied. "The last time they did this was when they attacked my mother's wagon train."

"So, they are the ones responsible for killing her parents and sister?"

"I'm afraid so."

"You must hurry, Takoda. Chief Matoskah is preparing the village for war."

"Thank you. Go back to the village and tell my father that I will be there very soon. I must set up protection here, but it won't take long."

Liwanu nodded and rode off at the same maddening pace as before.

Takoda turned to Sammie, whose face was as pale as a ghost. When he spotted Ellie in the doorway, he took her hand and then grasped her sister's. "We must hurry."

Leading them into the house, he instructed them on what to do. "Forget about the chores except for the livestock. I'll bring them extra water and food. Then, keep your doors, including the barn doors, locked tight, and cover the windows. Whatever you do, don't let the animals out of the barn. If they are locked inside, the warriors won't hurt them, but if they are running loose, they will drive them off or kill them for food. Store

180

food, blankets, and supplies in the hayloft for emergencies."

"But, Takoda, I can't climb…"

"I'll get the supplies up there and take care of the animals before I leave. And yes, you can climb. I'll rig up the pulley so you can slip into it, and Ellie can help lift you into the loft. You have strong muscles in your arms. I'll put it over the ladder so that you can pull yourself up as Ellie works the pulley."

"We can do that," both girls said.

"If raiders come, and you can't get to the barn, go into the root cellar. Have blankets, water, and supplies down there, as well." He lifted the hatch to the root cellar. "Yes, your father was wise; you can lock the hatch from inside."

"I'm scared," Ellie cried. "Don't leave us, Takoda!"

Sammie saw the conflict on Takoda's face, and while she too wished he would stay, she knew he had others to protect and broader responsibilities than the two of them.

"We'll be safe as long as we do what Takoda's told us to do."

"Both of you keep your rifles and plenty of bullets within reach at all times but don't shoot unless you must. Only to save your lives," Takoda continued. "Do you understand?"

"Yes," Sammie said, putting on a brave front for both her sister and Takoda's peace of mind.

"While I prepare the pulley and add some supplies to the loft, you get things ready in here," he told them.

Running outside to the barn, he began to set up everything to make the plan work. Taking the blankets, food, water, and supplies that Ellie had collected, he put them in the loft, brought in the animals, locked them in their stalls, filled the food troughs, and gave them fresh water. Then he closed the barn and headed back to the cabin. When he stepped inside, Sammie was handing supplies down to Ellie, who was in the root cellar.

"What else do you need down there?" Takoda asked.

"We're fine here." She rolled over to him and took his hand. "You had better head back to your village." Her eyes were filled with a combination of fear and worry, not only for herself and Ellie but also for him and his tribe. "Be careful. I know you have to fight. Just...."

Takoda lifted her from the chair, stood her on her feet, and took her in his arms. "I'll be careful. Do what I said. I will be back as quickly as I can."

"Promise...?"

"I do if you promise to keep safe for me."

She nodded, and the tears she had tried to hold back, began to flow.

Takoda held her tightly and kissed her lips, a long, slow kiss.

"Take care, my love. Keep safe, and I will try to do the same."

As he placed her gently back in the chair, he kissed the top of her head, then pulled Ellie to his side and kissed the top of her head as well.

They both followed him to the door and watched him ride away. Closing and locking the door with the new bar he had installed, she wondered if she would ever see him again.

# Chapter Thirty-Two

## War

When word reached the Shoshone village that the Comanches were once more on the warpath; every member of the tribe became involved in the necessary preparations to protect their home and people. But first, they held a meeting of all the men and the female elders.

"Our enemy is once more on the warpath," Chief Matoskah announced.

"They come to steal our horses and our food," one of the younger braves snarled.

"That may be so," the Chief agreed. "But they are also attacking the white settlements."

"Once again, we will be blamed for their warfare," a middle-aged warrior declared.

"Not by those who live closest to us. The white sheriff brought me this warning. He will make sure his people know who the enemy is."

"Ah, but to them, we all look alike," one of the women elders, added with a grunt.

"And there is no way for them to distinguish the difference between the nations. To them, a Shoshone looks just like a Comanche or an Apache or any other Indian," another agreed.

"Then we will have to be careful not to go near any of the white settlements," the chief said. "Let us prepare for war!"

Some of the women prepared war paint. The Indians believed that the designs they painted on themselves held magic powers of protection. They used specific colors and images to make their braves, and especially the chief, look ferocious and dangerous.

Although most Indian battles were short, they could be violent and bloody. One of the reasons for going to war was to protect the lives of family members from raiding war parties. The Shoshone people were not warlike by nature, but they would rise to the occasion when threatened, so it was necessary to increase the number of weapons they had.

Knives and hatchets were sharpened, and the men made new arrow shafts, which the women and older children fletched with three matched half feathers, equally spaced at the base of the shaft. Bows were whittled from sturdy wood and shaped in a double curve. A skilled warrior could release up to twenty arrows in under a minute. Spears were also carved from the hardwood found in the forest, smoothed and balanced to fly straight.

Extra food was gathered, prepared, and stored so that when the men were away at war parties, the women and children would not go hungry. They gathered seeds to grind into meal for making bread, as well as roots, berries, and pine nuts (small edible seeds of the female pine tree cone.) They had a buttery texture and were pleasantly sweet and delicious, as well as nourishing. Birds, rabbits, squirrels, ducks, grouse, and elk were hunted and prepared, much of it salted to preserve it from going bad.

The warriors of every tribe used stealth, camouflage, and ambush as their favorite means of attack. With the use of those skills, watchers also hid in trees and other secret places to warn the village of an approaching enemy.

As preparations were made, Rachel met with her husband.

"Takoda's woman," he began.

"I don't know that you could say she is his woman, though they care for one another. What about her?"

"I understand that she and her sister are alone at their parent's farm. They will need protection."

Rachel smiled and touched her husband's cheek. "Already you are thinking of them as part of our family, Matoskah. This is one of the reasons why I love you so. Takoda is there now, making preparations and instructing them, which is why he is late. Both girls are good with a rifle. With no one else to protect them, we must pray that what he is doing and their courage will be enough."

****

Bored by being cooped up in the house, Ellie looked out the front bedroom window for the twelfth time that day. She was about to turn away until something caught her attention. Puzzled, she continued looking until she realized that what she saw was dust rising from the road that led straight to their cabin. She watched until she could almost make out one of the riders.

"Sammie! It's Takoda! He's coming!"

Sammie ran to the window and looked out. The riders were still too far away to make out facial features, but it was apparent they were Indians. She grinned at Ellie. Then she quickly wheeled into her room to check her hair and pinch her cheeks for color. When she was satisfied, she hurried into the living room and was about to open the door, when over the hill; a dozen Comanches screamed and hollered their war cries.

There wasn't time to run to the barn without being seen. "Ellie, get your rifle, and as many shells, you can carry and go down into the root cellar."

"What about you?"

185

"I'll be down in a minute." When she saw her sister's stubborn expression, she said, "Please do it now. I'll be right down. I promise."

Sammie already had her rifle. She grabbed bullets and her mother's Bible, placing them both in her lap. Heading into the front bedroom, she realized her sister had not gone to the cellar but was right next to her. They peeked through the small opening at the side of the curtain. Despite Takoda having locked the barn doors, the Indians had still broken in. Some of the braves ran out carrying squawking chickens; another led Annabel by a rope looped around her neck. But Annabel wasn't making it easy. She kicked and bit the warrior in the arm, causing him to drop the line. Angrily, he lashed out at the normally docile cow, but before he could strike her, she jerked away and ran into the hills.

"Annabel!" Ellie cried.

Sammie put her hand over her sister's mouth. "Shhh. She got away. That's good. She'll come home once the warriors are gone," Sammie assured her.

"But they're taking our chickens, and Annabel needs to be here to feed her calf," Ellie whispered angrily. Determined, she checked her rifle and headed for the front door.

"No! Ellie stop! They'll kill you."

Sammie wheeled her chair swiftly and caught her sister by the arm, stopping Ellie before she could unlock the door. Jerking her into her lap, she whispered, "We can hand feed the calf and breed up more cows. I can't breed another you. And remember what Takoda said, 'no shooting!' "

Hearing the war cries growing louder, the girls realized the Indians were now circling the cabin, riding around it, and yelling even louder than before. They exchanged frightened looks and dared not look outside any longer.

"We need to get into the cellar before they see us," Sammie urged.

But as the words left her mouth, a flaming arrow burst through the window in their room. The curtains instantly caught fire, and then the bed, where the arrow had embedded itself.

"Ellie, grab the bucket of water from the kitchen."

As her sister ran into the kitchen, Sammie picked up the pitcher of water and tossed the water on the flames. It wasn't enough. Ellie hurried back, trying unsuccessfully not to spill any. Her sister handed her the pitcher. "Fill this up and toss it on the burning curtains."

As she did, Sammie threw enough water on the bed to finish putting out the flames. The last pitcher doused the flames on the curtains. There was no time to think. Two more flaming arrows stuck in the wood covering the front window. A fourth flew through the kitchen window and hit one of the living room chairs. Sammie grabbed a blanket and beat the flames out in the chair, but the board on the living room window was now wholly engulfed and spreading to the walls.

"It's no use!" Ellie cried. "We're out of water."

"Hurry, grab your rifle and bullets, and get into the root cellar. It's our only chance."

"But we'll die from the smoke and fire above us," Ellie cried. Both she and Sammie coughed as smoke began to fill the cabin.

"We have to get in the cellar right now. There's no way out where we won't be seen. Outside means death. The cellar will at least give us a fighting chance."

Tears ran down Ellie's face, but she headed for the root cellar. Before she got there, however, she was nearly overcome by smoke.

"Drop to the floor and crawl. The air is better there. Ellie went down to her knees and crawled toward the trap door. Sammie left her wheelchair, set the rifle, Bible, and bullets on the seat, and pulled herself along the floor to the kitchen, where she grabbed three dishtowels and dragged them through the spilled water on the floor. Pulling herself back to the trapdoor three feet away, she tossed Ellie her rifle and one of the towels, and then threw the ammo down to her, followed by the Bible.

"Put the towel over your mouth," Sammie ordered as she did the same. Then she reached for one of the wheels on her chair and rigged it to the trapdoor with the remaining towel. She climbed down the ladder using the strength in her arms, while Ellie held her legs against the rungs. When she pulled the door shut, the wheelchair fell over on top of it, blocking the door from view.

Both girls dropped to the ground, which they had earlier covered with an old rug. Neither one had been keen on sitting or lying in the dirt.

"Pour a little more water on our towels. It will make breathing easier."

Ellie did so, being careful to preserve most of the water. As they sat close together, breathing through the damp dishtowels, they were surrounded by noise. The Indian's war cries were somewhat dulled in the cellar, but the crackle and roar of the fire above them was growing louder.

Sammie remembered to lock the trap door, then reached out and held her little sister in her arms, rocking her as she cried and shivered with fear. She felt like doing the same, but she knew she had to stay strong for both of them. Fortunately, smoke rises, so the air was much better in the damp cellar, and they were able to stop much of their coughing.

Time seemed to drag by fueling Sammie's fears. If the cabin was completely engulfed in flames, the floor would also burn. Would the flaming debris eventually fall on top of them? She wracked her brain, trying to think of a way out. When nothing came to her, she began to pray, keeping the words inside her head for fear of frightening Ellie.

*Dear Lord, if ever we needed you, it's now. I am so grateful for all you have done so far. If not for Rachel and Takoda, I would not have been able to crawl from my chair and get down here, and I believe that you sent them to us. But Lord, we're trapped; our home is burning above our heads. We're surrounded by enemies with no escape in sight. Help us, please, save us. Ellie is too young to die, especially like this. And I, thanks to you, have the promise of a beautiful future with Takoda, one that I would never have dreamed of before. Please don't let all that has happened to be in vain. I ask this through your Son, our lord. Amen*

Sammie had just finished her prayer when a loud crash sounded at the front of the house. She heard angry voices and footsteps of several men on the floor above them. A new fear gripped her. If the attackers moved the chair or saw the trapdoor beneath it, they would probably smash it in. She and her sister would be as good as dead. Sammie held Ellie even tighter, and with her eyes, instructed her to be very still and quiet.

The house wasn't entirely on fire because she heard the sound of things being thrown on the floor and breaking. She listened as the Indians spoke to each other, but she didn't understand what they were saying. They finally left the cabin and rode away, shouting their victory.

It took a while before Sammie was convinced she was no longer hearing the noise of the invaders. Ellie, in her fear and exhaustion, had fallen asleep.

****

"Ellie," she said, gently shaking her sister. "Ellie, wake up. They're gone."

"How do you know?"

"It's been quiet for a while now. Help me climb the ladder."

Ellie clung to her fearfully. "But what if they aren't? What if they're still there waiting for us?"

Sammie shook her head. "If they knew we were down here, they would have come after us. I heard them ride away, and it's been quiet ever since. Come on, Ellie. We must be brave."

Ellie sighed and wiped her face with her practically dry rag. "Here goes nothing."

Sammie reached for the ladder and pulled herself to her feet. Ellie stood behind her one rung below. Thankfully, Sammie's arms were strong from all the years of pulling herself through the garden.

Feeling the trapdoor for heat to make sure the fire was out, she threw the lock, placed her hands and upper back against the hatch, and pushed with all her might. The wheelchair didn't fly off, but it scooted enough that she could grip the edge of the floor and continued pushing until the door swung free. When she poked her head out, it was difficult to see through all the smoke, even though it now escaped through the gaping burned holes in the roof and the front wall of their home. She coughed and covered her mouth with the dishtowel. Her eyes teared up from the smoke, and she hastily wiped at them. When she could finally see better, she gasped at the horrible scene before her.

# Chapter Thirty-Three

## The Aftermath

Sammie bit her lip, and silent tears rolled down her cheeks as she viewed the devastation surrounding her. The fireplace was the only thing remaining intact in the living room, but even its bricks were blackened with soot. Piles of ash and broken bits of wood were all that was left of their furniture in that room. Only the studs in the interior front bedroom wall, the front outside wall, and part of the outside wall on the right remained. And they, too, were blackened and charred like everything else. They stood like devastated sentinels, framing the exterior of grass, crops, and woodlands that surrounded the cabin.

The kitchen and back bedroom contained a few undamaged things that would help ease some of the trauma of their life while living in the barn. Still, the ordeal ahead would not be an easy one.

Her face was so wet, but then she realized it wasn't from crying. It was raining, which was a blessing, as it helped put out the remaining embers.

"What do you see, Sammie? Are the Indians gone? " Ellie asked. "How's our house?"

Pulling herself up the last few steps and onto the charred wooden floor, Sammie looked down at her sister. "Prepare yourself," she warned. "There isn't much left that wasn't burned, and it's raining."

When Ellie poked her head out and looked, she realized their home was gone and began screaming.

"No," Sammie warned, covering her sister's mouth with a hand. "Stop screaming. We don't know how far away those Indians are. They might hear you and come back."

Ellie's body was shaking, her eyes wide with shock, but she did not cry out or scream as Sammie pulled her up through the hole and into her arms.

She stroked her hair and rocked her.

"It's going to be alright."

"No," Ellie choked out the words, "It isn't. Our beautiful cabin, Mother's prized furniture, all our things…."

"Can be replaced." Sammie was a bit surprised at the words that came out of her mouth, but as she thought about them, she knew they were correct. "It looks like we can salvage several things from the kitchen: the sink, some dishes and pans, and two buckets, but there are more of those in the barn." She leaned left to look into their parent's room. "Ma and Pa's room isn't as badly damaged. The clothes trunk is scorched a bit, but it didn't burn. So, at least we won't have to run around in our undergarments."

That made Ellie laugh. Then she suddenly sat up straight and looked. "But Ma's beautiful couch and chairs and…."

"We're alive, Ellie, and that's all Ma and Pa will care about. Once the rain stops, we'll head for the loft in the barn. Tomorrow, we can start moving whatever we can salvage down there. There's an empty corner on the wall away from the animal stalls and chicken coup. We'll make our new home there until Takoda comes back. He'll help us rebuild the cabin. You'll see."

Ellie hiccupped. "He will…won't he?"

"Of course, he will. He's very clever with his hands, just like Pa."

192

"Do you still think Pa and Ma are coming back? Do you?"

"I don't know, sweetie, I hope so. With all my heart, I hope so."

*****

Since the girls had some provisions already in the barn, they took some clean clothing and a few small essentials to the barn. Too tired to think of food, they each had a glass of water, locked the door, and slept in the loft that night. Exhaustion and trauma were the only reasons they slept at all. The following day, Annabel returned. Sammie was as happy to see her, as the cow was to be back home with her calf.

"Oh, Annabel, my beautiful, beautiful girl, I knew you would find your way back to us."

The cow mooed and settled in to feed her hungry calf. If only they still had Gypsy. She would have made things a lot easier. The girls pulled out a low, four-by-four wagon and used it to bring everything they could salvage down to the barn. Ellie and Sammie in her chair pushed and pulled it back and forth between the cabin and barn. It took several trips, as they didn't want to overburden themselves. The sink went separately, as did their parent's mattress, the stove, and the trunk with blankets, linens, and things. The girl's trunk had several singe marks on the top and sides, but the rain had put out the fire before it burned completely through the wood. Their clothing was unharmed, and for now, they decided to keep them in the trunk until a new chest could be made.

It took all day until dark to move everything and set up a corner of the barn to make a temporary home. Fortunately, the food inside the root cellar was fine, as were the remaining crops in the fields. For some reason, the renegades had not set fire to the field, and Sammie sent up a prayer of thanks to God.

Ellie worked hard, chatting from time to time, but her infectious enthusiasm was missing. She didn't sing or play-act as she had in the past. Even her conversation was mostly about how to set up their temporary home and the things that needed to be done. By the end of the second day, the girls had set up an area for the kitchen. They used two bales of straw to hold up the sink and draped some others with tablecloths for stacking the dishes and pots. The area where the stove sat was cleaned out, removing everything flammable so that only the floor was under it.

A rope nailed to two walls, with a quilt thrown over the top, gave them privacy for sleeping and dressing, not that the animals would care. There was nothing they could do about the barnyard smell, and after a while didn't notice it much at all. That second night, after eating supper, the girls sat on the bed against the barn wall and talked.

"Ma and Pa are not returning," Ellie said quietly.

Sammie turned her head to look at her sister. "You say that like it's a certainty."

"Isn't it? If they were still alive, don't you think they would have come back long ago?"

"There still could be a perfectly logical reason for their delay. The doctor probably wants Ma to heal more before undergoing the trip back. Pa may have run out of money and had to take a temporary job to pay for medical treatments, room, and board. It could be anything."

"I used to think like that, too, but I was only fooling myself, and so are you."

"Why the sudden change? This lack of hope?" Sammie asked.

"Look around. We've lost almost everything. Since they left, everything that can go wrong has. We have worked so hard all summer, and for what? I guess you could say I've had to grow up and accept the truth. You need to accept it, too."

It was true. Since the raid and the loss of their home, Sammie noticed a definite change in her little sister. It was a loss of innocence. It broke Sammie's heart that her thirteen-year-old sister had to mature quickly due to all the tragedy they'd had to endure. Of everything they'd lost, however, it was the fact that their parents might never return that hurt the most.

"I'm sorry, Ellie. It shouldn't have happened like this. Still, it isn't hopeless. We could have lost the barn, too. We could have lost our lives. At least now, we have a chance to rebuild and continue. There's still a lot of life to live."

"Sammie, Sammie, Sammie, face reality. You don't have to pretend for my sake any longer. My fairytale world and dreams of happy endings are gone, lost along with my childish imaginings. Don't get me wrong. I still want more than ever to become an actress. It's just that now I see it through different eyes. I'm no longer a child. Let's go back to New York City and live with Grandmother. We can give the cows and the remaining chickens to Takoda and Rachel. It's not like we're abandoning them or leaving them to fend for themselves. The Shoshone people will take good care of them."

Sammie shouldn't have been shocked by her sister's proposal, but she was.

"No, that's impossible. We need to stay here and rebuild for Ma and Pa, for when they come back. When this Indian war is over, Takoda will return and help us. You'll see."

"What if he doesn't make it back?" Ellie asked.

Sammie knew that was a possibility, but she refused to accept it. She prayed several times a day that God would keep him safe and bring him back home to her. She was gaining strength in her legs, determined to get stronger and walk so she could help him rebuild the cabin and hoping, with all her heart, they could build a life together.

"Even if he does come back, the house won't be ready until sometime next year. We'll have to spend the winter in this awful barn. We'll probably freeze to death!"

"Ellie listen...."

"No! You listen. Do you like it here? Now? I make believe I can't smell it, but I can't ever get that awful stench out of my nose, even when I'm outside. I'm sick of it! I'd be ashamed to have anyone come near me because my clothes, my hair, even my skin smells like dung."

Sammie opened her mouth, but then she closed it. Ellie was right. She knew in her heart her sister was right, but she couldn't leave. *What if Takoda doesn't come back? What if he is killed? Then what are you going to do?* What if her parents don't return? She would have no choice but to return to New York. "You promised you would stay until the end of this year."

Ellie's shoulders sagged. "I did, and as much as I don't want to, I will honor that promise, but not one day longer. It's almost time anyway. I've never liked the farm. You know that. And now, I hate it even more."

# Chapter Thirty-Four

## Trapped!

It had been a week since the fire. Even Sammie had to admit it would be nice to at least sleep someplace where the air was fresh and clean. That wasn't an option. It would be too dangerous to sleep outside and, eventually, too cold. They often ate outside, however, just to get away from the constant smell.

Around mid-afternoon, Sammie sat in her wheelchair in front of the open barn door. She hadn't slept well the night before and, after several hours of hard work, needed to rest a bit before going on. Having dozed off, she was unaware that the trapper, riding the horse he had stolen from them, had entered the property and sat, mostly hidden by a copse of trees, surveying the charred skeleton of the cabin.

The sight of the cabin's burned-out husk angered him. It interfered with his well-laid plans, which had been to take the farm for himself and make the girls do all the work. Having witnessed their parents' wagon as it washed downstream, he believed they were dead. So the girls were alone. Dugger could have rebuilt the cabin, but he was too lazy to do that much work.

Turning away from the cabin's remains, he looked at the barn and spotted Sammie sitting there asleep. Then a cruel smile lit his features. *If I can't have the farm, I can still get some money for those girls.* Leaving his hiding place, he rode casually toward the barn.

Sammie didn't know if it was the clip-clop of the horse's hooves or the sense of danger that awoke her, but her eyes popped open. Seeing the trapper riding down the trail toward her, she quickly rolled into the barn and grabbed her rifle.

"Ellie, grab your rifle and go up to the loft. Dugger is coming. If he gets past me, you'll be in a good position to shoot him if necessary."

Ellie's face turned white. She was a good shot after all the practicing she'd done, but she wasn't sure she could shoot another human being. Still, she knew the danger, so she quickly followed her sister's instructions.

Sammie headed back outside and aimed her rifle at the trapper, who was still fifty yards away. "That's far enough." She fired a shot that zipped over his head. "That was a warning shot, now get off my property, or I'll shoot you dead and feed your carcass to the coyotes."

"You got quite a mouth on you, Little Sister." Nevertheless, he was shaken by how close the bullet had come to plowing a furrow across his head. He brought his stolen horse to a standstill. "Injuns do that to yer cabin?"

"None of your business. And while you're at it, get off my horse and send him back here."

Dugger eased the horse forward at a slow pace. He did not dismount, however.

"Stop right there!" Sammie raised her Winchester rifle a little higher and chambered another bullet. "I won't ask again."

He reined in the horse, bringing it to a halt once more. "Look, with all the raidin' going on by those renegades on the loose, I just thought I'd check up on you and your sister. It looks like it's a good thing I did, what with your house burned down and all. Can't be livin' in a barn for the rest of yer life; it ain't healthy. Could freeze t' death."

"Like I said, it's none of your business," Sammy hollered back.

"Why don't you two come with me? I can get you work in the mining town a few miles ahead. They need women to cook and clean and wash clothes for the miners."

"You're kidding, right? You want us to become maids?"

"Ain't all that bad, at least you'd have food in your bellies, a solid roof over your heads, and some money in your reticule. And who knows, you may decide even to marry one of those miners down the line. After all, it's the least I can do for stealing your horse."

"I have food and a roof over my head, and I'd have money in my purse, except you stole it all," Sammie snapped.

"Where is that sister of yours anyway?"

"She left for New York to live with our Grandmother. I'll go there myself before I'd ever agreed to become somebody's maid. I'm a farmer, not a maid."

"Well, Miss High and Mighty, I got word on your parents," Dugger taunted.

Sammie lowered her rifle a bit, allowing him to come closer. "Well, out with it."

"Your parents are dead."

"Liar! You're a liar and a thief. Get off our land, you no good cowardly liar. And stay off, or I'll shoot you right off that stolen horse!" She quickly raised the rifle and shot at him as he turned and galloped toward the hills.

He grinned and shouted over his shoulder, "Saw 'em drown with my own two eyes. You're all alone. No Ma. No Pa. Nobody."

Another bullet whizzed past so close it nicked his ear. He left, angry and mumbling, "You've not seen the last of me, Little Sister."

"Next time I won't give you a warning shot!" she screamed after him. As he disappeared over the horizon, her anger gave way to fear. *Please, God, no. He's a liar. I know it. Nothing but a dirty liar. Ma and Pa are okay. They'll be back, and so will Takoda. We'll all be all right. Right, God? Right?*

*****

The following day, Ellie was at the lake getting water. As she plunged the heavy bucket into the water, she heard a branch snap. Ellie glanced around on the alert for a wild animal but didn't see any. Then she had another thought.

"I hear you, Takoda. Instead of creeping about trying to frighten me, you could come down here and help with this bucket. It's heavy and hard to fill."

Frustrated, she let out a sigh and was about to call out to Takoda for help again, when a large, dirty hand clamped over her mouth and jerked her backward. Ellie dropped the bucket on the ground. Eyes wide with terror, she grabbed frantically at the hand, trying to pry it loose, but she couldn't budge a finger.

Pulled against her attacker's chest, his other hand went around her waist. Ellie struggled, but her kidnapper lifted her off the ground and carried her towards the woods. She kicked and jabbed with her elbows, but the arms only tightened around her.

"Be still. Stop!"

Ellie stiffened in the attacker's arms. She knew that voice. She couldn't quite place it, but she was sure she had heard it before.

"I'm going to take my hand away from yer mouth now, but if you let out so much as a squeak, I'll tie your jaw shut so tight, you won't be able to breathe. Got that Little Sister?"

Ellie nodded her head as best she could, tears spilling down her cheeks. What was happening? As the hand slowly pulled away, she lunged, trying to take a bite out of it. She missed, however, and he slapped the back of her head so hard; she almost passed out.

"No funny business. No screaming, talking, kicking, or biting. Try any of that, and you'll be in a gunny sack in no time at all."

Ellie clamped her eyes shut and tried to calm herself. Then slowly, she opened them to look into the most fearsome, sneering grin she had ever seen. "You!" she whispered. "What do you want?"

"Oh, not much; just you, Little Sister. I know this nice family in…where's that town now? Somewhere far off, looking for a house servant."

The thought of being sold into slavery was too much. "Sammmieeeeeee! Help!" Ellie jerked her head away and yelled with all her strength. "Saaammmmiieeee!"

Sammie heard her sister's calls for help. *What now?* She wondered. *That girl can turn even getting water into a drama.* But when she heard Ellie scream her name a second time, she rushed to the barn door. Something was very wrong.

Pulling the door open, she rolled her chair outside. *Where is she?* The screaming had stopped. "She went to the lake for water, so where is she?" she said aloud. She turned toward the lake. Sammie scanned the area, frowning at the sun.

"Ellie! Ellie!"

Silence.

She looked again, squinting, searching. She heard the hoof beats first, then breaking into her line of vision, a dark horse, a rider, and Ellie.

"Ellie!"

Her sister was lying across the saddle, screaming, Sammie's name over and over.

The rider kicked his horse into a gallop. Then turning toward the hills, Sammie watched Dugger ride out of sight.

*Dugger!*

Sammie's chest tightened painfully. She couldn't save her sister, even if she still had Gypsy. It would have taken too long to get back to the barn and saddle the horse. He would be long gone before she even rode out of the barn. But, she didn't have Gypsy, he did, and now he had Ellie. Her hands became fists.

"No! No! No!" she screamed in frustration and anger. Helpless in this horrible chair. She pounded her fists on the wooden armrests, and remembered, with anguish, the trapper's terrible last words, *"You're all alone. No Ma. No Pa. Nobody."*

It was growing dark. Sammie returned to the barn and built a fire outside in front. She looked up at the stars and prayed. When she ran out of words, she read her mother's Bible. It was all up to God and her faith now. With nowhere else to turn, she closed her eyes and then opened them. Something strange came over her. Her faith, which had slowly been deepening, grew monumentally stronger.

"He is a good and loving God." Looking up at the brightest star in the sky, she said, "I know you will return all my loved ones to me. I know you will send Takoda back. I believe this with all my heart and soul." She looked down at the fire and whispered, "I believe."

# Chapter Thirty-Five

## Takoda's Quality

Sammie felt sick to her stomach all night as she thought about her terrified sister and what the trapper might have in mind for her. She figured he would sell Ellie into slavery since that would get him the most money. The idea filled her with dread. She knew her sister would rebel, which would lead to a punishment that could be severe, depending on the temperament of her owners. She just prayed that Takoda would come back quickly and save Ellie before anything like that happened.

Too nervous and upset to just sit and wait, Sammie practiced the exercises for her legs, pushing herself to near exhaustion. As she worked and exercised, she prayed and read from her mother's Bible. By now, she knew several passages by heart. She repeated these over and over in her mind whenever both hands were busy with work.

**\*\*\*\***

Two more days passed, but she kept the belief that God would answer her prayers and save her sister. Sammie did not know if she was still in danger from the renegade Indians, but she decided to put the cows in the pasture next to the barn. Going back inside, she fed the chickens and grabbed a bucket to fetch water, even if it was only half a bucket at a time when she heard a rider approach. Grabbing her rifle, she quickly wheeled out of the barn, thinking Dugger might have come back for her. Once outside, she raised her gun and looked up the road.

"Takoda!" The name left her mouth the second she realized who it was. She lowered the rifle and wanted to run and meet him. The fact that she couldn't nearly made her scream in frustration.

Gingerbread trotted up, and Takoda dismounted with a grimace. He looked around and saw the burned-out husk of the cabin. Then he looked at Sammie. Instinctively, he knew by her expression that there was more wrong than just her destroyed home.

"Did the Comanches do that?" he asked, pointing to what was left of the cabin.

"Yes."

"What else?" he asked alarmed when Ellie did not come out to greet him.

"Ellie...he...he took her." Sammie's words were punctuated by hiccupping sobs, as for the first time, she allowed herself to break down.

"Who, the renegades?"

"No." Sob. "Dugger." Sob. "Kidnapped her."

He squatted down in front of her chair, and she leaned forward and hugged him until she heard him grunt with pain.

"You're hurt," she exclaimed.

"Two broken ribs. Tell me what happened."

Sammie told him about Dugger's visit and the kidnapping the day after. "I've been praying and praying for your safe return and for Ellie. But you can't go looking for her like that, injured, with broken ribs."

"I have suffered worse. I cannot delay. Dugger already has a two-day lead. Hopefully, Ellie is slowing him down. Come, we'll ride Gingerbread to the lake, so I can examine the area where he took her."

Sammie opened her mouth to protest, but one look and she decided that words would be a waste of breath. When they reached the lake, it was easy to see where Ellie had been snatched. A patch of ground near the lake was trampled heavily. Nearby foliage showed signs of an animal having grazed there recently, while other spots showed signs of a struggle. Slipped off his horse, knelt on one knee, and carefully examined the areas.

"Hmm, Ellie fought him."

Sammie leaned forward in the saddle. "How can you tell?"

"There are some blood spots. Here...," he said, pointing to several leaves of the trampled plants. "And here."

Sammie's stomach knotted. "How do you know that's not Ellie's blood?"

"The blood is splattered here, here, and here." He grinned up at Sammie. "I'll bet she bit him. Dugger would not risk hurting her. She would lose value when he tried to sell her." Takoda stood up and walked back to the spot by the lake. "Here's where she stood to fill the bucket with water. See the indentation in the mud?"

Sammie urged Gingerbread a little closer, careful not to trample any clues. "Yes, I see it."

"The bucket was too heavy. Ellie dropped it, spilling some of the water back into the lake. Ellie must have stomped her foot in irritation here," he said, pointing to a small footprint deeper than the others in the mud. "She refilled the bucket and was lifting it when she was taken."

"How can you tell?" Sammie was so perplexed that she had stopped crying.

Takoda pointed to a spot a few feet away along the bank. "There is your bucket, hung up on that branch." Turning, he moved back to the second disturbing area. "There are two sets of footprints back there. Then the small prints disappear, and the larger prints are deeper from this point on. No doubt, he picked her up and carried her struggling to his horse."

He looked at the nearby trees and foliage and pointed to a mark on one of them. "She must have made this scuff mark with her shoe during her struggle. Then once more, we see two sets of prints – one large and one small, and signs of a struggle. Then only the large prints remain by these hoof prints. This is where he most likely threw her across his horse and rode away."

He tracked the marks made by the hooves, while Sammie followed along on Gingerbread. At one point, two sets of tracks intersected, then split, one going off in the direction Dugger would have had to take for Sammie to see him ride off with Ellie.

"He rode in from that way," he said, pointing to the tracks that led to the area. "I'll take you back to the barn and go after him."

When they arrived at the barn, he dismounted and lifted Sammie from his horse, setting her gently in her wheelchair, and grimacing from the pain it caused to his ribs.

Sammie reached out and grabbed his hand. "Let me go with you," she begged.

He shook his head sadly. "You will only slow me down. My mother will come as soon as she finishes mending our wounded."

Sammie knew better than to beg. She did not want Takoda to think less of her, especially since she knew he was right. She would have to leave everything to him and God. "Wait; let me send some food with you. I know you can hunt for your food, but it will take the time you won't want to lose."

Takoda smiled at her. "You know me well, but please hurry. I must follow their trail before it is lost."

Sammie quickly gathered some biscuits, dried venison, that Takoda had supplied before leaving to fight the Comanches and some fruit. Tying it up in a cloth, she handed it to him, and he attached it to his saddle.

"Be brave, White Dove. I will find Ellie and bring her back to you." He kissed her, then jumped on his horse and rode off, following the trail left by Dugger's horse.

"God be with you," Sammie called. Then lowering her voice, she added, "Please, God, go with him and help him save my sister."

**** 

Since two days had passed, tracking Dugger wasn't easy. Besides his tracking skills, Takoda had to think like the trapper. He figured the outlaw would believe that no one would follow him, so he took the most comfortable way back to civilization. Takoda prayed for guidance, and after a moment of quiet contemplation, he headed off in what he hoped was the right direction – down a trail, over rocks, through shallow water, and up a mountain.

He saw enough signs along the way to know he was on the right track, especially when he discovered Dugger's day old camp and the remains of his fire. The pain from his broken ribs was like a constant toothache, but he continued onward, not even stopping at night to sleep. He was grateful to Sammie for providing him with food. It enabled him to eat while he rode and kept up his strength. His mother had bound his ribs with strips of cloth back at the village before he'd left to see Sammie. It helped him breathe a little easier.

On the evening of the first day and far into the next, it began to storm. The rain came down in sheets, making it difficult to see. Lightning streaked down the sky from the heavens in bright jagged spears that looked like tree branches, followed by thunder so loud it would have spooked many horses. But Gingerbread had been trained to ignore the loud cracks that boomed through the air. Takoda continued onward, and that evening as the lightning and thunder faded away, and the rain slowed, he discovered Dugger's camp.

There was no campfire, thanks to the rain. Takoda rode silently as close to the camp as he dared. Ellie was tied to a tree trunk. Dugger slept under the spreading branches of another tree not far away. Dismounting, Takoda slipped up to Sammie's stolen horse, speaking quietly he soothed the animal and untied him. Then he slipped over to Ellie and covered her mouth with one hand.

Her eyes popped open, and she tensed, expecting to see the trapper. Instead, she saw Takoda putting one finger to his lips. She nodded to him, her eyes large and round with fear of discovery. Takoda removed his hand from her mouth, pulled out his knife, and quickly cut the ropes binding her to the tree. Then he stood up, lifted her into his arms, and carried her back to his horse. Placing her in the saddle, he took the reins of both horses and quietly led them away from the camp. They were about twenty feet away when a bullet whizzed past them and hit a tree.

Ellie screamed, and Takoda jumped on Gingerbread, behind Ellie, and hit the rump of Sammie's stolen horse.

"Ya!" Gypsy took off running, and Gingerbread followed, both horses galloping through the dangerous woods at breakneck speed.

Dugger fired at them until he emptied his gun.

Ellie held onto Gingerbread's mane with both hands, as Takoda urged him onward. She concentrated on hunching over and being small and compact, as the Indian's horse galloped through the woods. They were getting away! Suddenly she felt Takoda's weight on her back, and then a warm wet liquid penetrated the fabric covering her left shoulder. Takoda had been shot.

"Takoda, you're hurt," she cried.

"No matter what happens," he told her, his voice barely above a whisper, "Stay on the horse. He will take us home."

# Chapter Thirty-Six

## The Final Showdown

Dugger was furious. "That dadgum Indian! I got em' tho. I can forget about that sister. Horse'll probably take her back to his village. But, he'll be dead before sunrise. Still," he stopped and squinted, thinking, *Another sister is ripe for the pickin'*. He rubbed his scruffy beard. She'll *never hear me comin'. Don't know what I'll do with a cripple, but I'll figure it out.*" As he rode toward the farm, his plan started to take more shape. *Maybe I will rebuild that cabin, after all, the land's worth somethin'. Just keep lame little sister to run my new farm. Shoot, once I get that gun away from her, she'll be my new little cook n' housekeeper. Who knows what else she's good at,* he laughed. Dugger had it all figured out.

*****

Sammie moved from her chair to the bed. She sat with her back against the wall and hugged her drawn-up knees. Tired of the battle and of God ignoring her cries for help, she sat alone and afraid. *Alright, God, I believe in you, but you don't care about me, about Ellie, about Takoda. So what good are you?* She cried. For a moment, anger flared up within her. She grabbed her mother's Bible from the top of a wooden crate she used as a nightstand and threw it. As soon as it hit the ground, a loud crack of thunder sounded, making her jump.

A new storm front, worse than the earlier one, was moving in. Sammie pulled herself back into her wheelchair and went outside in the nearby pasture, trying to get Daisy, Annabelle, and her calf back into the barn. The two cows were happy to get out of

210

the storm, but Butch, who was still a young calf, was in a playful mood. She tried to grab the rope around his neck to lead him inside, but he was too fast, and she kept missing. As she wheeled her chair toward the barn door, it got stuck in a puddle of mud, and no matter how hard she tried, she couldn't get it unstuck. So she pulled herself free of the chair, calling Butch as she crawled through the mud, pulling her chair by one wheel toward the barn.

Butch finally ran inside to his mother, which was a relief, and Sammie went inside after him, locking the door behind her. She removed the rope from the calf and carried it over to a hook outside Gypsy's empty stall.

Sammie was wet right down to her undergarments, her clothes covered in mud. She cleaned as much mud from the chair as she could, then threw the dirty rag on the floor. Days earlier, she and Ellie had hauled in enough water to fill the metal tub they used to bathe. Exhausted and defeated, Sammie stripped off her filthy clothes, and with great difficulty, pulled herself into the metal tub. Without her sister's help, she couldn't heat the water, so she was forced to take a cold bath. Her mud-caked clothes would have to wait until she could go to the lake and wash them.

Sammie, chilled from the cold bath, forced herself to wash until the water turned murky and even colder. As she struggled to pull herself out of the washtub, she felt so alone and depressed. All she could think about was Takoda and Ellie and wondered if they were alive. She didn't feel like sleeping, so instead of pulling on her nightgown, she dressed in clean underclothes and a new dress. She also slipped a knife up her long sleeve. It was a habit she had formed since moving into the barn. Then picking up one of the books she managed to save from the fire, she parked the chair near the bed and began reading. She was just about to turn the page when a knock sounded on the barn door.

*That must be Takoda returning with Ellie,* she thought excitedly. And because she felt that she did not grab her rifle. Smoothing her hair, which was still a little damp, she pinched her cheeks and wheeled over to the door. She threw back the lock and opened the door—her welcoming smile and the words that had been on her lips melted away.

Dugger stood there, sneering at her.

Sammie wheeled backward as fast as she could, and when the trapper stepped inside, she threw her book at him.

He laughed. "Surprised to see me, Little Sister?"

"Where's Ellie?" she demanded.

"You don't need to worry about her. She's someplace where she'll never get away," the trapper lied.

Sammie turned her chair and started wheeling toward the bed. The trapper looked at the bed and saw her rifle lying there. He sprinted toward it, grabbing the Winchester just before she got there.

"Oh, no, you don't, Little Sister. Say, this is a mighty fine rifle. This your Pa's?"

Sammie remained silent.

"I think I'll just have to keep it. I've always wanted a repeating rifle. It's too good for a woman, anyway."

As he reveled, Sammie let the knife slip down her sleeve and into her hand. She raised it to stab him, but he caught her movement out of the corner of his eye. Dropping the rifle, he turned and backhanded her so hard that the knife flew out of her hand, and her wheelchair was knocked over as she tumbled out and onto the barn floor.

He snarled. "Think you're pretty brave, don't ya?" He righted the chair and retrieved the knife, which he then stuck, point outward, between the spokes of one wheel, keeping the chair in place. "Now, we'll just wait for your Indian friend."

"Why? What makes you think he'll come?"

"Actually, I'm hoping he doesn't cause that'll mean he's dead. You see, I shot him while he was trying to rescue your sister."

Sammie wanted to scream, cry, and lash out. Anger won. She wouldn't let him see her cry. She was about to crawl over to her chair, but then she thought better of it. If she crawled, he would know she had some strength in her legs. She wanted to seem completely defenseless. It was better to save that surprise for a time when it might be more useful. So she dragged herself toward the chair, hoping to pull the knife out of the spokes and throw it at him.

It was like he could read her mind. Grabbing her under the armpits, he half carried, half dragged her to the wheelchair, and slammed her into it. Sammie's frustration increased because the only way she could pull the knife out of the spokes was from the inside, under her chair, which meant she had to be on the ground to do it.

She wanted to give him a real piece of her mind, let him know she wasn't afraid, and he would eventually become her victim. However, she thought against it, knowing he would only laugh at anything she might say. She did, however, give him such a nasty look that if looks could kill, he would be lying dead on the floor.

Dugger retrieved the rifle and sat down on a bale of hay to wait. Thirty minutes passed, and his stomach rumbled. "I'm getting mighty hungry." He stood up, removed the knife from the spokes, and stuck in his belt. Then he went to the makeshift kitchen area and grabbed up the remaining sharp knives, which he stuck high up into the wall of the barn. "Fix me some supper, and a strong pot of coffee."

"We're out of coffee."

"Don't try foolin' with me, Little Sister, I...."

"I'm not fooling!" She shouted back. "See for yourself."

Dugger rummaged through the boxes and burlap sacks in the make-do kitchen. There was no coffee. He turned to Sammie and started to say something when he heard a horse's whinny on the other side of the barn door. Cautious, he pulled his gun and eased over to it. He listened, but all he heard was a horse, which was now pawing at the door with his hoof. It could be a trap. When nothing further happened, he eased the door open a bit, ready to shoot whoever was out there. Gypsy stuck his nose in the opening and pushed.

"Well I'll be," Dugger said as he opened the door wide enough to let in the horse. "Look who wants in. Did you miss me, fella?"

Gypsy snorted and headed straight for Sammie.

"Good boy," she said as she stroked his nose and laid her head against his muzzle.

"Ain't that sweet," Dugger sneered. "You're just in time." He reached into one of the saddlebags and brought out his small supply of coffee, which he tossed to Sammie. "Get busy."

Sammie tried to buy time so she could think. Slowly she made the coffee and put together some supper, while Dugger walked Gypsy over to an empty stall, unsaddled, fed, and watered her.

"Lookie here. Did you manage to clean out this stall all by yourself? He turned and looked at Sammie. "I doubt it. An Indian doesn't just help a woman for no reason. He grimaced. "What's the world comin' to, a white woman taking up with some dirty renegade?"

"He's not a dirty renegade. His people are peaceful, and he's a good friend who's been helping out with the chores until Ma and Pa return."

"I told you. They ain't comin' back. They're dead."

"I don't believe you. You're just sayin' that to scare me. You're not only a thief but a liar, too!"

"I saw their wagon get washed downriver with them in it. I saw it with my own eyes."

"I still think you're lying. And even if it were true, that doesn't mean they're dead."

"Wagon's not a boat. It was half sunk before it went round the bend. And your Ma was in no condition to swim. She would have sunk like a rock. Your Pa most likely died tryin,' like a fool, to save her."

Sammie looked away. What he said made sense. She couldn't bear to think of her parents drowned. Her grief was stifling. However, she would not cry and give him satisfaction. Biting her lip, she fought back the tears until she once more had her emotions in check.

Dugger sat down at the makeshift table. "Quit moping around. Is my dinner ready yet?"

Sammie prepared him a plate and handed it to him. "Do you want your coffee now?"

215

"Course I do. Need it to wash down this grub, don't I?"

Grabbing a cup, she handed it to him and reached for the pot. Dugger wasn't ready for what happened next. Using a folded hand towel, she picked up the pot and started to fill his cup, but before it was even half-full, she shifted the stream of hot coffee and poured it in his lap instead.

Dugger yelled, dropping both the cup and plate. Burned and enraged, he grabbed her knife out of his belt and threw it at her.

Sammie pulled the knife from the bale of hay where it landed. Then quickly wheeling to the lantern, she blew out the flame, throwing the barn into pitch blackness. She had been in the barn so often, especially since living there, that she knew her way around even in complete darkness.

"You gonna run over me with your wheelchair, Little Sister?"

Sammie knew better than to answer. It would give her position away. Listening carefully as he tried to make his way through the darkness, she heard him run into the stove and banged his knee badly.

"Dagnabbit! Where's that, lantern? Once I find it, I'm going to take care of you once and for all!"

The words had barely left his lips when he was hit in the legs from behind with the wheelchair, knocking him over. Sammie hurriedly rolled away, unknowingly running over his arm, until she felt a bump and heard him yelp.

"Ha! That'll teach you to make fun of my wheelchair," she goaded him. *Now, where did he put my rifle?* She searched her memory, trying to recall where he had set it down when she handed him the plate of food. *It must be somewhere in the kitchen area.*

While she searched for the rifle, Dugger stumbled and felt his way towards what he hoped was the barn door. He didn't, however, remember how she had set up the temporary living arrangements.

"Ba bawk!"

"Dang chicken, git out of my way!"

Now all the chickens were squawking and flapping around, surrounding him. Confused by the darkness and the stranger, their agitation grew, making it even more difficult for the trapper to get away as they pecked at his legs. Sammie's eyes adjusted to the darkness, and while the chickens kept Dugger busy, she spotted her rifle and quickly snatched it up. Aiming for the sound of his voice, she fired off a round as the trapper tripped over a chicken. The fall saved his life.

"Good thing for me; you can't hit the side of a barn. Or in this case, maybe you did," Dugger laughed as he crawled toward the spot where he saw the muzzle flash. Sammie wheeled away. Then using the top of the gate, she stood up and slipped inside Gypsy's stall. She reached over and gently laid her hand on his mouth so he would remain quiet. It was a trick she had taught him years ago.

Dugger knew she had moved, but he wasn't sure where she was. Getting to his feet, he drew his pistol and cautiously stepped forward. He was so angry now; he didn't care if he killed her or not. He would still have the farm and its livestock. And though he, too, could see a little better, had no idea where she was hiding. Once more, he tried to orient himself and headed for the barn door. It was still dark outside, but the storm had stopped, and the moon, which was full, would provide the extra light he needed until he could find that lantern and relight it.

His hands extended, he walked forward slowly. And when his hands found the barn wall, he grinned, his thoughts cruel and evil. He kept following the wall until he found the door, which was still unlocked. Before throwing it open, he put his back to it and fired several shots in different directions, peppering the barn with bullets, aiming waist-high, since he thought Sammie was still in her wheelchair.

One bullet went right through the door of Gypsy's stall. Sammie bit her lip to keep from crying out. She did not want to get shot, but she was also worried about the livestock. When the shooting stopped, she inwardly sighed with relief. The animals were all safe. She knew this because if one had been hit, it would have cried out.

Dugger turned and threw open the doors. The shots he had fired were meant to keep Sammie off balance, and it worked. As the moonlight filtered in through the doorway, Sammie slipped from Gypsy's stall, leaving it open a few inches so as not to make any noise. Then she grabbed the coil of rope off the hook, got into her chair and headed for a trap door in the floor of the barn partially hidden by the straw.

Sammie dropped to the floor and pulled more straw over the door. Then open it, she shoved the chair away from her and dropped down inside, lowering the lid as she did.

Hearing the noise, Dugger came back into the barn and quickly found the lantern, which he relit. He was surprised when he saw the empty chair in the middle of the floor. "Hiding are we Little Sister? Won't do you no good. Now that there's light in here, I'll find you. And then I'm gonna teach you a lesson."

A jolt of fear raced through Sammie. Slowly, she inched the trapdoor open just enough so she could peek out. His back was turned to her as he grabbed her chair and pushed it outside the barn. "Won't be able to go nowhere, now that your wheelchair is out of reach. You cooked your goose, Little Sister."

Sammie grimaced. She had grown to hate being called 'little sister.' She watched him search the barn. When he turned her way, she eased the trapdoor shut, cocked her rifle, and waited. Waiting quietly, she thought about Ellie and Takoda.

What had happened to them? Did Takoda really find Ellie and rescue her? Did Dugger shoot Takoda? No, that was one of his lies. Then where was he? Where was Ellie? She didn't know what to believe. But, she made a vow to find and rescue her sister, even if it took her the rest of her life.

For the first time, Sammie did not feel helpless. She could actually move her legs and even stand for a short time. The exercise had worked. That, along with Takoda's encouragement, she no longer felt trapped in her chair. She wanted to think more about Takoda and Ellie; try to figure out what happened, but she had to focus.

Alone, in the dark, she prayed, *I'm sorry God. I'm not mad at you. I believe you can help me.* Suddenly she had clarity and strength and no fear. She also had a plan. So, she waited.

While Sammie waited for the right moment to capture the trapper, Dugger finished searching the barn. He was surprised when he didn't find her in one of the stalls. He was sure she would be hiding there. Moving back to the other side of the barn, he glanced around once more, a puzzled expression on his face. *Maybe she slipped out of the barn while my back was turned,* he thought. He turned and looked outside the barn door. No, the wheelchair was still there.

"Where are you, Little Sister? You can't hide forever. I'm gonna find you one way or the other, so you might as well come out and surrender."

Sammie heard his footsteps draw closer. She locked the door as quietly as possible, but it still made enough noise that he turned his focus to the floor where he heard the sound.

*Is that a crack in the floor?* He hurried over and brushed some of the straw aside. A smile of triumph lit his face as he grabbed the handle and jerked upward. The trapdoor rattled but did not open. "Got yerself locked up in there, do ya? Well, I can fix that in a hurry."

Taking the lantern, he quickly searched the barn. When he didn't find what he wanted, Dugger went outside and looked around until he found the woodpile and chopping block outback. Grabbing the ax, he hurried back inside and set the lantern down. "Better watch yer head. Ax comin' through!"

Sammie scooted to the furthest corner and tried to roll herself into a tight ball, her head as low as possible.

*Bam!*

The ax bit into the wood above her, but it wasn't enough to break the lock.

*Bam! Bam! Bam!*

With the last swing, the trapdoor flew open. Sammie swung the rifle up. But before she could pull the trigger, Dugger reached inside, grabbed her gun and her arm, and dragged both out. He threw her to the floor, but Sammie sat up and looked up at him, without an ounce of fear. She crawled to the side of the broken trapdoor.

"Where do you think yer going? Ain't nowhere left to hide. Yer finished."

Sammie smiled at him.

"You addled or somethin'? Whatcha smiling at?"

"You."

Hearing a sound behind him, Dugger whirled around, thinking it was the Indian. Then he smiled. "Get back to yer stall, ya lousy fleabag," he told Gypsy.

The horse stood almost on top of him, and as soon as Dugger called him a fleabag, Gypsy gave him a rough push with his head, knocking the trapper headfirst into the open hole.

Sammie caught the rifle as it flew into the air and pointed it at the trapper-now lying unconscious at the bottom of the hiding space. She poked him with the barrel of the gun to make sure he wasn't playing possum. Dugger was out cold. Then standing up, she hugged her beloved horse. "Good boy, Gypsy."

Gypsy nodded up and down and let out a loud horse laugh.

"We'd better get him out of there and tied up real tight." With the rifle still cocked and pointing at the trapper's head, she lowered herself next to him, grabbed the rope and tied it around the unconscious trapper twice, firmly pinning his arms to his sides. Relieved that he was still unconscious, and she didn't have to shoot him, Sammie climbed out of the hole. She made a loop on her end of the rope and put it around the horse's neck. "Pull Gypsy. Good boy. Good boy!"

Once Dugger was pulled free of the trap, she led the horse over to one of the barn posts and removed the loop from the horse's neck. With another long length of rope, Sammie tied the trapper's ankles together and drew them up so that his feet were above his hips. Finally, she wrapped the rope around and around the post as many times as it would go and secured the end. He looked like a fat caterpillar in a cocoon.

"That should keep you for a while."

*****

When Dugger awoke, he struggled to get free, but it was no use. So he sat there, trussed up like a holiday pig, and stared daggers at Sammie, who was in her wheelchair, her rifle across her lap, staring right back at him.

"You may as well relax until someone comes," Sammie said, remembering that Takoda had told her his mother would be there once she finished treating the wounded villagers. "There's no way you're getting out of that."

"You have enough rope on him to secure at least four men," a voice said behind her.

"Takoda! Ellie!" Sammie eased herself to her feet and turned to find, Ellie, Rachel, and Takoda standing there.

"You're standing!" All three cried.

"Oh, Sammie." Ellie hugged her sister tightly, and Sammie returned the hug with all her strength.

"I'm so glad Takoda found you."

Rachel also hugged her. "I am so happy you're safe," then looking at the trapper, "And so proud of you." With one more gentle squeeze, she stepped back to allow Takoda to take her place.

The couple embraced for a long time. Seeing the new bandage and remembering his broken ribs, Sammie was cautious not to squeeze him too tight. Above all, she wanted to look into his eyes, so she lifted her head from his shoulder, and he kissed her.

"I love you so much. I was terrified I had lost you," Sammie told him.

"And I love you more than life. The whole time I've been gone, I prayed for your safety. God has answered both our prayers."

# Chapter Thirty-Seven

## Home At Last

The following morning, another stranger appeared on the farm.

"Sammie, someone's coming!" Ellie shouted. "They're on horseback."

Ellie ran to the barn door as Sammie wiped her hands on a dishcloth, and rolled outside, just as the Sheriff and two deputies were dismounting their horses. Sammie wore brown leggings that Rachel had made for her, under her dress. They were so comfortable. Her hair was now cut shorter, just below her shoulders. Takoda said he loved how it swung carefree whenever she rode. Sammie was more confident than ever. Takoda, who was brushing Gypsy in the stall, stayed inside.

"Morning, Miss, are you Samantha McPherson?" The Sheriff asked.

"G' morning Sheriff. Yes, I am, and this is my sister Elizabeth. How can I help you?"

The Sheriff looked at Ellie, removed his hat, and gestured to the two men with him. "My deputies," he said. "Mind if we come in for a spell?"

"Of course. Since the Comanches burned down our home, we've been living in here," she led them into the barn. "Come Spring; we'll rebuild." She turned her chair around as the men observed the makeshift home.

"This is Takoda,"

The Sheriff and his men smiled as they shook hands with Takoda "No need for introductions, Miss Samantha, we're good friends with Takoda, and his pa, the Chief. Nice to see you, son."

Sammie knew there had to be more of the story but now wasn't the time.

"I'm sure you could all use a glass of water after the long ride in from town."

"I'll get it." Ellie jumped up and went to the makeshift kitchen.

"I'm sorry I don't have anything but hay bales to offer as seats. We lost everything in the fire, but what you see," Sammie informed him.

"After the long ride out here, we're quite happy to stand thank you. That's a right shame about your home," the Sheriff told her. "I'm mighty sorry that happened."

Ellie handed out the water. The men accepted their glasses and tipped their hats to her.

"I imagine you came to pick up this man," Sammie said, pointing to the trapper who was gagged and securely tied to a barn post. "Takoda said he sent a messenger to let you know we had him, but I didn't expect you so soon."

The Sheriff took a good look at the trussed-up man. "I know this no-good yella dog." He shook his head at the trapper, "Well, Dugger, it looks like your criminal career is over." He turned to Takoda, "Who captured and hogtied him, you?"

Takoda smiled and shook his head as he walked over to Sammie, "No, Sheriff, I did not. Sammie did. Captured him all by herself and did that fancy rope tying as well. It's very secure. You will probably have to cut him out of there."

The Sheriff looked at her in amazement. "You did this?"

"Yes, sir." She blushed, then looked at the trapper, who seemed harmless all tied up.

"Well, he stole my horse over there," she said, pointing to Gypsy, "Ma's jewelry, and other things from us. He also kidnapped my sister and threatened to kill me." She

225

frowned with intensity, "I think you'll agree. He needs to go to jail."

"Miss Samantha, he has a high price on his head. He'll go to jail alright, and then most likely be hanged. He's more than a thief. He's wanted for murder."

"*Murder*? I didn't know. I guess God protected us."

"I would say so." He took another look at the scowling, cocoon wrapped Dugger, and turned back to Sammie. "You all right? He didn't hurt you, did he?"

"No, sir, he didn't have a chance."

"Well, I'll be." He and the two men laughed, looking at Sammie with a new sense of respect. "Well, Miss Sammie, I'll be sure you get that reward – it's a good sum of money."

\*\*\*\*\*

A few days later, Sammie, Ellie, Rachel, and Takoda sat around a large wooden table in the barn, crafted by Takoda. They were having dinner when they heard a wagon approach.

Before anyone could move, Ellie jumped up and ran through the open barn door. When she saw who it was, she forgot everything and everyone in the barn and ran down the road.

"Ma! Pa!"

Her words brought everyone to their feet and through the barn door.

When Ellie reached the wagon, her pa brought it to a halt and reached out his hand to help as she climbed on board. Her mother, seated beside her husband, wore a brace but paid no mind to it. She opened her arms to her youngest, smiling and laughing as her daughter kept kissing and hugging them.

Sammie and Takoda stood together, his arm around her back, along with Rachel as the wagon pulled up. The minute Ben saw his eldest daughter between two Indians, he pulled out his rifle.

Ellie reached out and pushed the rifle barrel down. "It's okay, Pa. That's our friend, Takoda, and his Ma."

Ben lowered his rifle, looked at Ellie, and then back at Sammie. Then it hit him. His eldest daughter was standing! "Ellie, Sammie is standing. How…?"

"Oh, Pa, we have so much to tell you! Like I said, that's Takoda, right there." She pointed, smiling at the tall, handsome Indian. "After you left, he watched out for us. He knew we were alone, so he watched us."

"He watched you?" Ben looked with concern at Ellie.

"Like a big brother. It was tough for us to do some of the chores. He brought us wood, and fixed the porch steps, and well, helped us so much with the farm and all. Oh, and that's his mother, Beautiful Moon, but we call her Rachel. See, she's dressed like an Indian because she's married to the Chief. She's not just a healer; she's also a doctor!"

"Well, well, well," Ellen said with a smile, enjoying every bit of Ellie's enthusiastic monologue and trying to keep it all straight. She reached over and squeezed Ben's hand and nodded her head.

"Go on, Ellie, what else? "

"She helped Sammie get better with exercises and swimming. But Takoda made her ride a horse first."

"What?" Ben was more confused than ever.

"And Ma…." Ellie turned with eyes filled with joy. "Ma, she prayed for Sammie.

That's the real reason she can stand. She prays to Jesus, just like us. And she prayed with me every night, and read Bible stories, and took care of me when I was sick."

Her mother's smile quickly turned to a frown. "Sick?"

"Oh, I was sick with whooping cough. I thought I was going to die. Really, that's the truth. She came and took care of me, brought me medicine, and did I tell you she prayed for me?" Ellie jumped down from the wagon. "Come on, come on. You gotta see how we're rebuilding the cabin. It's gonna have another bedroom and a bigger porch. You see, after the bad Indians, the Comanches went on the warpath, and burned it down, we moved into the barn. It's okay once you get used to it, but we made it nice inside. Then when Takoda got better from his broken ribs and from being shot by Dugger."

"Dugger? The trapper - big man, with a longish beard, gold tooth?" Pa asked.

"Yes!" Ellie interrupted, pleased that her Pa was finally understanding. "He was really bad. He tricked us and stole Grandma's necklace and Gypsy!" Ellie's eyes were as big as saucers. "And me... He stole me! Kidnapped me!"

Ellen's face went pale as she realized all the information she had fed the trapper, thinking he was a friend.

"But Takoda saved me. He found me, even though he got shot by Dugger. He found me and brought me home."

"And the trapper...what happened to him?" Ben asked.

"Oh, oh!" Ellie jumped up and down. "That's the best part!" She whirled around extended her arm in a dramatic gesture, like an actor would do at the end of a play, as she looked at her sister beaming, "Sammie captured him and tied him up. The Sheriff said 'like a hog,' and the Sheriff came and got him, and then we got some reward money. The

Sheriff told if they didn't hang him, he'd be in jail forever and ever!"

Ben and Ellen just looked at each other, confused, amazed, but so happy to see both their girls unharmed, healthy, and thriving. They tried to take it all in; the charred remains of their home next to a new structure being raised, their daughter standing, the beautiful blonde woman dressed as an Indian, the Indian with an arm protectively around Sammie. It was too much to comprehend.

Benjamin jumped down from the wagon, walked around to the other side, and carefully lifted his wife down next to him. Speechless, they walked up to Sammie. Takoda released her, and she took two slow steps toward them. Benjamin ran up to her and lifted her in his arms, laughing with joy. Then he pulled his wife to his side, embracing both in a huge hug. Ellie jumped up and down and danced like an Indian around them.

"Sammie and Takoda are getting married," Ellie sang out.

Sammie shot her a warning look, but she was being squeezed so hard by her pa, she just had to laugh.

When Benjamin finally put Sammie down, Ellen turned toward Rachel, who was standing quietly to one side. "Come," Ellen said with a smile as tears ran down her cheeks.

She opened her arms to Takoda's mother and pulled her into the circle. Takoda stepped forward and slipped his arm around Sammie's waist. Then he reached for the dancing Ellie, pulling her to his other side.

"Thank you, Rachel, for taking care of our girls when we couldn't. You are the angel we prayed for."

"Thank you." Benjamin turned to Takoda and stuck out his hand. "I can't even begin to imagine the real story behind all this, but I suspect you had a large part in it."

Rachel smiled and pointed toward the barn. "I'm sure you're hungry from your journey. Let's go inside. There's plenty of rabbit stew and cornbread, and I think we may need to fill in some of Ellie's story and hear about your journey. I believe God has been watching over all of us."

As the family sat around the beautiful table, Benjamin looked at each one. "Let us ask God to bless this food, bless our family and friends, and thank Him for all that He has done." Bowing their heads, he led them in a prayer of thanksgiving.

"Lord Jesus, we come to you in humble thankfulness. Thank you for protecting my family. Thank you for healing my wife. Thank you, God, for Rachel and Takoda, and for bringing them to help our girls. Thank you for strengthening Sammie's legs, and thank you for Ellie's joy." There was a pause, and then he continued in a softer voice. "God, forgive me for ignoring you all these years, and now for accepting me, despite all that I've done to keep you away. Please give me the wisdom I need as I lead my family. I commit myself and my family to you to serve you. And Lord, tomorrow as we face a new day, a new life together, lead us in Jesus' name. Amen."

"Amen." They all said.

"I wonder what will happen tomorrow," Ellie said. "I'm going to pray for a new adventure."

"Oh, Ellie," her mother laughed, "How wonderful to be part of your exuberant joy once again!"

That night after Takoda and Rachel left, all the stories had been told, and

Sammie's parents had accepted Takoda as their daughter's suitor. Sammie lay on a bed of hay in the dark, waiting for sleep to come. She thought about the past several months and all the pain and sorrow, happiness and joy they had lived through. She and Ellie had grown and changed a lot during that time, as had their faith in God.

"I'm so sorry I ever doubted you," Sammie whispered in prayer. She remembered praying for help, and how He had answered her by sending Takoda. What a fantastic way to answer my prayer, she thought with a smile. "God, you know how to love us so perfectly, and how to send love to us. Thank you for Takoda. Thank you for answering my prayer beyond what I ever could have imagined."

She thought about all the things she had learned about her mother as she'd read her journal, and the marked verses in her Bible; the note her mother had written tucked away in the back of her dressing table, asking God for someone special for Sammie who loved God. *There were a lot of answers to our prayers, dressed up and disguised in ways we missed, especially me.*

"Despite all my doubt, all my mistrust, you never left us. And even in our times of fear, sickness, and trouble, you remained at our side. Thank You, Lord."

With those final words of prayer, Sammie's eyes closed for the night. For the first time since it had all begun, she felt safe and slept peacefully, never to feel alone again.

Spring was in full bloom, the temperatures were mild, and the new house was finally finished. Some adjustments, based on their growing family, had been agreed upon and made as Benjamin, Takoda, and after hearing their story, a few townsfolk worked together to have the exterior finished before winter. The rest was completed over the winter by Ben and Takoda. Two large bedrooms and one medium-sized bedroom, along with a private bathing chamber, graced the new house. There was also a larger living room and kitchen with plenty of room for the more prominent family. The reward money had come in handy. Although some furniture was ordered from back East, the men worked hard, building new furniture to replace the pieces destroyed in the fire. They also had to create a little extra for the bedroom the newlyweds would share later.

Besides the things they needed for the house, the family purchased more chickens, pigs, some cows, and a bull. They also enlarged the barn, and Takoda gifted Sammie and Benjamin, each with a new horse, since the two on the farm were more workhorses than riding ones. He had told Benjamin it was his tribe's tradition to give a horse to the future father-in-law. It wasn't, but Ben didn't know, and he accepted it graciously. It was the most exceptional horse he'd ever owned.

Ellen made new curtains, while Rachel and Sammie wove blankets. The two mothers also worked together on a beautiful quilt as a wedding present for the couple.

The wedding was held outdoors at the Shoshone village. Ben had written to the minister in Aspen, and he had agreed to perform the Christian ceremony, which was interwoven with many Indian traditions.

Baskets and pottery were decorated with ornate symbols and filled with food and supplies for the couple's new life together. A pottery jar with a handle on each side and two spouts, called a 'wedding vase', was filled with herbal tea. The couple drank from each side as a toast to their union.

Because her mother's wedding dress had been destroyed in the fire, Sammie wore Rachel's wedding dress. She felt so beautiful in the white, knee-length buckskin dress, rubbed and treated to be 'as soft as a bride's smile.' Long strings of white fringe hung from the voluptuous sleeves, as well as the hem, and along with a V shape on the front and back above the waist. A belt of turquoise and white beads graced her waist, and she wore a matching beautifully the turquoise and silver necklace around her neck. Ellen made her daughter a wedding bouquet of spring flowers tied with blue and white ribbons. Takoda wore new white buckskin pants and a shirt with turquoise and white beads and turquoise and silver jewelry, and finely decorated wedding moccasins.

They were a beautiful couple in their wedding finery. But what everyone commented upon were their faces; they shone with such love and joy that some of the older Indians said 'the gods smiled upon them with unfiltered adoration.' Sammie, with her new-found faith, and Takoda, walking with the God he'd known and loved since a child, understood that God, the God of the Universe, had truly blessed them – and they were happy.

That day, the McPherson family officially became members of the Shoshone village. It was a beautiful ceremony. Of course, Ellie was beside herself with excitement in a fawn-colored Indian dress, with feathers and beads strategically woven in her braided chestnut hair. As the "maid of honor," a term the tribe knew nothing about, she assumed

233

her duties with such high spirit and exuberance, and she quickly won the hearts of the Shoshone people.

Rising Moon, Takoda's sister, adored being a 'bride's maid,' another unknown Americanism. Dressed in a slightly darker dress than Ellie, to offset her blond hair and fair skin, the Indian girl was delighted to honor her brother and new sister-in-law in this American tradition. She walked proudly, beautifully, as a true Indian princess, knowing every young brave had her eye on her. But, she was saving her heart for one warrior in particular.

Everyone ate a large sumptuous meal prepared by the women of the village. The wedding cake, another American tradition, was a labor of love between Ellen and Gertrude. Who came all the way from Aspen with her husband, the doctor, and the Pastor and his wife, to be a part of Ellen and Ben's happiness. It was by far the most beautiful treat, a white cake with three tiers, and covered in Ellen's buttercream icing. Ben had carved a wooden bride and groom out of soft pine and stained it with whitewash. Many years later, Sammie's great-granddaughter would use it on her wedding cake. The Pastor married the couple and gave a rousing sermon about Jesus coming to save all the people on earth, and that in heaven, there would be only one great tribe, with one great Chief.

The newlywed couple was given their tent, where they spent their wedding night. It was small and intimate, with a small fire already burning in the center. This was the Shoshone tradition, and Sammie thought it was absolutely beautiful and romantic. However, they both knew they wanted to live on the farm where they would work the land and raise horses and cattle. It was a rich, deep heritage, for they would enjoy the benefits, and be welcome, in both worlds, as would their children.

The ceremony lasted late into the night. There was much dancing, both Indian and American, one teaching the other, as the music ricocheted back and forth. It was a celebration that was talked about for many years, each generation adding its own extra flourish until it became a legend.

*****

As spring moseyed into summer, Takoda helped Ben ready the fields and did the planting. A more extensive pasture was cleared and seeded for the additional livestock, and so the horses Takoda raised could be brought to the farm.

Throughout the warm summer days, Sammie and Takoda worked on the garden together. He helped her by supporting her, not in the wheelchair, but as she made small baby steps. After lowering her to the ground, they worked together side-by-side. Ellie joined them one day, bringing a harvest basket. She plopped down beside them and worked at pulling weeds.

Takoda was startled when a small animal ran up and jumped into Sammie's arms.

"Why, Mrs. Rabbit, how are your babies today?"

As if to answer, the hare looked back as several pink noses poked above the rabbit hole.

"You brought the whole family? Just don't eat all my carrots," Sammie laughed.

Life was heavenly. Sammie's husband held her whenever she swam, and her muscles continued to grow more reliable and more durable. In the evenings, she studied the medical books Rachel had loaned her. She also learned all about Indian medicine, how to make herbal medicines and salves, and other healing ways. Sammie's desire to become a doctor was being fulfilled in a very different way. Since she was married to the

Chief's son, her mother-in-law was happy to pass on the Indian traditions, and as they worked side by side, Rachel discovered that Sammie had a unique gift and love for healing. Rachel knew someday, her daughter by marriage would replace her. And this pleased her very much.

Sammie saw how physical therapy strengthened her legs, and so she used some of these techniques to help her mother, who also grew stronger and healthier. Baling hay in the barn loft was left to the men now without anyone saying a word.

*What a life I've lived, and am living,* thought Sammie. God had given her so much. So, one evening she began writing a journal. Perhaps God could use her story to help or encourage someone else. She was very transparent and truthful, so she wrote carefully about those months of anger, confusion, and trials, and how she became a stronger, fearless woman, as she opened her heart and life to God, the Creator that made her and understood her.

One evening, she sat in bed, writing that day's entry. Tired, she leaned back against her pillow and headboard and fell asleep, pen in hand, and journal open to the last page.

When Takoda came into bed, he smiled at the beautiful woman who was now his wife. Gently, careful not to wake her, he took the pen and laid it on the nightstand, closed the inkwell, and placed a kiss on her lips. Then he slipped the journal from her hands and read her last entry.

"We are never alone."


-The End-

www.ingramcontent.com/pod-product-compliance
Lightning Source LLC
Chambersburg PA
CBHW031322170626
46807CB00002B/523